The
Golden Day

The
Golden Day

URSULA DUBOSARSKY

CANDLEWICK PRESS

Dedicated with great affection
to my own class of 1978

The author would like to thank the following for permission to use quoted
material: page 56, excerpt from the song "Joy Is Like the Rain" (1966) by
permission of the author, Miriam Therese Winter; page 127, extract from
Ancient History 3U HSC Examination Paper, copyright © 1976 Board of Studies
NSW for and on behalf of the Crown in rights of the State of New South Wales.

First U.S. edition 2013

Library of Congress Catalog Card Number 2012947715
ISBN 978-0-7636-6399-5

13 14 15 16 17 18 BVG 10 9 8 7 6 5 4 3 2 1

Printed in Berryville, VA, U.S.A.

This book was typeset in Perpetua.

Candlewick Press
99 Dover Street
Somerville, Massachusetts 02144

visit us at www.candlewick.com

Fear it has faded and the night:
The bells all peal the hour of nine:
The schoolgirls hastening through the light
Touch the unknowable Divine. . . .

Get thou behind me Shadow-Death!
Oh ye Eternities delay!
Morning is with me and the breath
Of schoolgirls hastening down the way.

——"Schoolgirls Hastening"
JOHN SHAW NEILSON

CONTENTS

1967

1975

The chapter titles in this novel are taken from paintings and drawings by Charles Blackman.

1967

"Let It All Hang Out"
The Hombres

ONE

All on a Summer's Day

THE YEAR BEGAN with the hanging of one man and ended with the drowning of another. But every year people die and their ghosts roam in the public gardens, hiding behind the gray, dark statues like wild cats, their tiny footsteps and secret breathing muffled by the sound of falling water in the fountains and the quiet ponds.

"Today, girls," said Miss Renshaw, "we shall go out into the beautiful garden and think about death."

The little girls sat in rows as the bell for morning classes tolled. Their teacher paused gravely. They gazed up at her, their striped ties neat around their necks, their hair combed.

"I have to tell you that something barbaric has happened today," said Miss Renshaw in a low, intent voice. "At eight o'clock this morning, a man was hanged."

Hanged! Miss Renshaw had a folded newspaper in her hand. She hit it against the blackboard. The dust rose, and the little girls jumped in their seats.

"In Melbourne!"

In Melbourne! They did not really even know where Melbourne was. Melbourne was like a far-off Italian city to them; it was Florence or Venice, a southern city of gold and flowers. But now they knew that it was cruel and shadowy, filled with murderers and criminals and state assassins. In Melbourne there was a prison with a high wall, and behind it in a courtyard stood a gallows, and a man named Ronald Ryan had been hanged at eight o'clock that morning.

Hanged . . . Who knew what else went on in Melbourne? That's what Cubby said. But Icara, who had been to Melbourne with her father on a train that took all night, shook her head.

"It's not like that," she said. "It's just like here, only there aren't so many palm trees."

Trust Icara to notice something peculiar like palm trees when people are being cut down on the street and carried away and hanged, thought Cubby.

Miss Renshaw beckoned at the little girls to leave their seats and come forward. They gathered around her, their long white socks pulled up to their knees.

"What did he do, Miss Renshaw?" asked Bethany, the smallest girl in the class. She had small legs and small hands and a very small head. But her eyes were luminously large. "The man who was hanged?"

"We won't worry about that now," said Miss Renshaw, avoiding Bethany's alarming stare. "Whatever he did, I ask you, is it right to take a man and hang him, coldly, at eight o'clock in the morning?"

It did seem a particularly wicked thing to do, the little girls agreed, especially in the morning, on such a warm and lovely day, when everything in it was so alive. Better to hang a person at night, when it was already sad and dark.

Miss Renshaw banged the newspaper again, on the desk this time. The little girls huddled backward.

"So today, girls, we will go outside into the beautiful garden and think about death."

Miss Renshaw was nuts — that's what Cubby's mother said. "Still, you've got to do what she says, Cubby. Remember, she's the teacher."

"But what if she tells us to jump in the river seven times to cure us of leprosy?" asked Cubby, thinking of the Bible story that one of the senior prefects, Amanda, had read out loud in chapel.

And Eli'sha sent a messenger to him, saying, "Go and wash in the Jordan seven times, and your flesh shall be restored, and you shall be clean!"

Up rose the voice of Amanda like smoke from behind the wooden eagle upon which the large Revised Standard Version of the Bible was laid out. Amanda's name meant "fit-to-be-loved" in Latin; Miss Renshaw had told them so. She was fit-to-be-loved, with her long, fair plaits as thick as the rope that the deckhands threw to tie the ferry to the wharf on the trip home from school. Everyone admired Amanda, and not only for her hair.

"Well, one step at a time," said Cubby's mother. "Let's wait and see if you get leprosy first."

Now Miss Renshaw stepped forward, leaving the newspaper on the desk. Miss Renshaw was tall, noble, and strong. Her hair was red and springy. She was like a lion. She stood at the classroom door, waiting while the little girls found their broad-brimmed, blue-banded hats, in preparation for leaving the safety of the school grounds.

Theirs was a very small class. There were only eleven of them, like eleven sisters all the same age in a large family. Cubby, Icara, Martine, Bethany, Georgina, Cynthia, Elizabeth, Elizabeth, Elizabeth, and Elizabeth, and silent Deirdre. Because it was such a very small class, they had a very small classroom, which was perched right at the top of the school. Up four flights of stairs, way up in the sky, like a colony of little birds nesting on a cliff, blown about by wind with the high, airy sounds of the city coming up the hill in the ocean breeze.

"Girls!" called out Miss Renshaw, smoothing her springy hair as they ran to tumble down the stairs, sixty-seven steps in total. "Hold hands and do not run."

Cubby grabbed Icara's hand, just as she had on the very first day she had arrived at the school, terrified and alone. Cubby preferred Icara to Martine or Georgina or Cynthia or Bethany or Deirdre or Elizabeth or Elizabeth or Elizabeth or Elizabeth, although the last Elizabeth wasn't so bad; she had a little brother who couldn't walk and had to go to a special school on a special bus and once Cubby had been to her house when her little brother was home, and they had pushed him around the garden in his wheelchair and how he had laughed as he threw back his thin neck, laughing out loud like a kookaburra.

The little girls moved in a cloud down from the classroom through the playground, to wait, as they had been taught, hand in hand at the yellow gate that led out to the big world. Miss Renshaw moved among them across the stone pathway. She wore a drooping crimson dress with a geometrical pattern of interlocking squares and triangles in green and purple. Around her neck on a string of leather swung a tear-shaped amber bead that glinted in the sunlight.

"Now, girls," said Miss Renshaw, "no screaming, squealing, or screeching. Remember, outside these walls, you are representing the school."

She turned the latch. The gate swung open with the softest creak, and out they ran, eleven schoolgirls in their round hats with their socks falling down, hand in hand, like a chain of paper dolls.

Miss Renshaw strode majestically at the rear in her droopy geometrical dress. She had no trouble keeping up with them, even though she was old. Of course, she wasn't as old as some of the teachers in their school. How frightened Cubby had been on her first day — she had never seen so many old women!

Their hair was white and gray or even yellow, and they smelled of ancient perfumes and powders and cigarettes. One teacher was so bent over she was like an old washerwoman from a fairy tale, her face always to the ground, scuttling off into the dim linoleum-floored hallways with books under her arm, muttering to herself. Another wore a net in her hair — Cubby had never heard of such a thing — and several had buns piled on top of their ancient, powerful faces, like African women in books bringing home pitchers of water from the well.

The little girls ran down the back lane behind the school, between the stinking mounds of rubbish and gurgling drains. They ran by sleepy, barefooted men and half-dressed women smoking on their doorsteps, and along the short wall outside the smudged church that lay under the shadows of the towers of flats. Their black shoes clattered one after another down the sandstone stairs, heading for the trees and bubbling water of the Ena Thompson Memorial Gardens.

"Wait!" boomed Miss Renshaw as they reached the edge of the street. "Do not cross until I say so!"

Cars rolled by. A dog was barking. They bumped together on the footpath, waiting.

"Stand still so I can count you," said Miss Renshaw. "Have we lost anyone?"

Across the road above their heads rose the tangled fence, with swirling metal words painted in gold in the shape of an arch. A glistening spiderweb dangled down from the *M* of *Memorial*. Miss Renshaw held her hand up in the air, her long fingers waving like pale streamers.

"Ten, eleven. Bethany, your hat is dirty. Elizabeth—yes, you, Elizabeth—pull up your socks. Cubby, your shoelaces are coming undone. I don't expect to take such grubby little girls into a public place. Remember why you are here."

Why were they here? They frowned at one another. Oh, yes, to think about death. . . .

"Look both ways and cross carefully."

Cubby bent down to tie her laces. With her head upside down, she caught sight of the water through the fence and the greenery, patches of the great Pacific Ocean rolling in icy steel-gray waves, beyond all the yachts and ferries and rowboats, on through Sydney Harbor, on and on all the way to Tahiti, all the way to the Sandwich Isles, thought Cubby, where Captain Cook sailed on his little boat and was eaten up.

"Wait for me, Icara!" shouted Cubby, straightening up, seeing Icara skip across the road through the warm, purple-smelling air. She could feel her lace was still undone but there was no time to stop and fix it now.

"Icara! Cubby! Stay together!" called Miss Renshaw after them.

Wait for me.

TWO

Into the Beautiful Garden

THEY ALL KNEW, even tiny, big-eyed Bethany knew, the real reason Miss Renshaw wanted to go out into the gardens that morning. It was not to think about death. Miss Renshaw wanted to see Morgan.

Morgan worked in the gardens. They had met him there one day when they arrived with pencils and sheets of blank paper to do drawings of leaves for natural science class. Morgan had been sitting under the great, creaking fig tree by the seawall, his back against the trunk, his eyes closed, smoking a cigarette.

"Like Buddha under the banyan tree," said Miss Renshaw later, "waiting for enlightenment."

Was it enlightenment? Or was it the noise of the children that made Morgan open his eyes? He had beautiful eyes — soft, brown, wet with tears, like a stuffed toy. He stubbed out his cigarette and stood up, tall in his muddy boots, blue shirt and trousers, and a floppy gray hat.

"Good morning, ladies," he said, putting his hand to his dandelion-soft beard.

The little girls wandered away. They were not interested in Morgan. But Miss Renshaw was. She leaned against the seawall with him, and they looked out at the Pacific Ocean and Morgan told her all about himself. Morgan worked in the Ena Thompson Memorial Gardens, mowing the lawns, pulling out weeds, planting flowers, trimming bushes, sweeping paths, cutting branches from the trees, keeping the water of the duck pond and its wedding-cake fountain clear of weeds.

Morgan was a poet as well as a gardener, Miss Renshaw told them later, when they had returned to the classroom.

"I knew he was a poet," Miss Renshaw said, "before he even opened his mouth to say good morning."

"How did you know?" asked Georgina curiously.

Miss Renshaw didn't say. She just knew. Miss Renshaw loved poetry.

"And even more than poetry, I love poets," avowed Miss Renshaw. "The person who has said 'My life is to make poetry' is a brave person."

"Why brave?" asked the tallest Elizabeth.

"Because poets are poor," said Miss Renshaw.

"Why are they poor?"

"People need poetry, but they won't pay for it," Miss Renshaw explained. "The great hope of a poet, girls, is to find a patron. Someone who will provide them with money and even a haven of peace and tranquillity while they write their poetry."

"Like a husband," suggested Georgina.

"In some ways," conceded Miss Renshaw, a little frostily.

"Why do you need money? Is it very expensive to write poetry?" asked Cubby, puzzled.

"It's hard to have a job when you're writing poems," said Cynthia in a worldly sort of way.

Why? wondered Cubby, although she did not say so out loud. Her father took the train to work and back every morning and evening, twenty minutes each way into the city. He could write a poem every day on the train in both directions. At that rate, he could write ten poems a week.

But not Morgan. Morgan was a real poet—poor, handsome, clever, and even famous, Miss Renshaw said, if you spoke to the right people.

"Are his poems in books?" asked the oldest Elizabeth.

"Morgan is widely published," said Miss Renshaw evasively.

"Can you write poems too, Miss Renshaw?" asked Bethany, with her big eyes.

"We can all write poems," replied Miss Renshaw, "if we allow ourselves. But we need to feel free to write poetry. We need to stop thinking of the facts, and think more about our feelings."

"Let it all hang out," agreed Cynthia.

Cubby pictured the family washing on the clothesline in

the backyard — shirts, skirts, shorts, and underwear, spinning in the wind.

"How do you write a poem?" asked long-haired Elizabeth, tossing her tight black plaits back over her shoulders.

"Aha!" said Miss Renshaw. "Now, that is the question. You need to get out of here to write real poetry. You need to get away, outside these walls, these floors."

She stamped her foot on the linoleum beneath them, splotched with old chewing gum and the remains of crawling insects. She stamped on the overhanging gloom of indoors, the narrow benches, the damp bricks, and the chapel of hidden windows, wood and brass and cloth.

"You must look up into the sky, open your minds, your eyes, your hearts! Poems will appear in the open air!" Miss Renshaw cried. "You need to reach out and grasp the words from the sunlight. Most of all, you must stop thinking. That's the real secret. Stop thinking."

How? thought Cubby. *How can you stop thinking?*

"We must get away from this place," said Miss Renshaw, shaking her springy head. "Away from this school, this institution. Then we can find true poetry. To go far, far away into nature, grass, water, the huge sky, and the deep brown earth."

Although, not that far, it turned out. Just as far as the Ena Thompson Memorial Gardens. Back they went, several times, with pencils and sheets of lined paper, to write poetry. Miss Renshaw did not write any poems, though, not that they saw.

"Run away, girls," Miss Renshaw would say as they passed

through the archway into the gardens. "Go and listen to the running water, then pick up your pencils and write a poem about it. I will stay here in the shade and talk with Morgan."

Obediently, gladly, the little girls would run away through the heavy-branched trees and careful rosebushes, across the samples of grasses from South America. They would stand and listen to the bubbling fountain, and the clip-clopping of the ducks as they paddled about the glossy pond.

This was just the sort of thing you should be able to write a poem about. But when Cubby listened to the fountain, it only made her think of the broken cistern in the toilets under the gym, mossy and dank and smelling like a dead body mixed up with old cartons of rotting milk. You couldn't write a poem about that, could you? Although Icara said you could write poems about horrible things just as much as beautiful things.

"Did Miss Renshaw tell you that?" asked Cubby, feeling doubtful.

"I don't need Miss Renshaw to tell me how to write a poem," replied Icara scornfully.

Icara and Miss Renshaw did not get on.

"Miss Renshaw doesn't like me," Icara told Cubby.

"Icara is too much of an individualist," Miss Renshaw would say with a sigh, which usually meant that Icara disagreed with Miss Renshaw.

"We're enemies," said Icara.

"Why?" asked Cubby, alarmed. Enemies? Enemies were countries, tanks and planes, soldiers in uniforms with helmets and guns, not ordinary people in classrooms.

Icara shrugged. "I don't know," she said. She didn't seem to care particularly. "It might be because my father is a judge."

It was true: Icara's father was a judge. He sat in court in red robes and a white wig and sent people to prison. Or worse. No wonder Miss Renshaw didn't like Icara. After all, it must have been a judge who decided that Ronald Ryan was to be taken away and hanged until he was dead.

"Miss Renshaw hates me," said Icara.

"We must work together for the common good," Miss Renshaw declared one morning. "Icara is too reserved. *Reserved* is a synonym for *distant,* which is a synonym for *far, far away.* What is another word for *far away?*"

This was a kind of game. Miss Renshaw would say a word and see how long a chain of similar words they could make.

"*Remote,*" said Georgina.

"*Isolated,*" said Elizabeth with the plaits.

"*Far-flung,*" said Cynthia through a mouthful of pink meringue she was secretly eating underneath the desk, and that was the end of the chain; nobody could thing of anything else.

Far-flung, wrote Miss Renshaw on the board in yellow chalk.

Far-flung

Miss Renshaw had large, round, sloping, marvelously neat blackboard writing. Nobody could write on the blackboard like Miss Renshaw. "Icara is far-flung."

But with Cubby, Icara was not far-flung. She was nearby-close-at-hand-a-stone's-throw-away. They were friends without either of them really knowing why. It was as though after that first day, when Icara had taken hold of Cubby's frightened hand, she had never let it go. Cubby and Icara could sit together in the playground or on the bus or in the library not saying much for hours, just a lovely rhythmic silence, like the sound of breathing when you're asleep.

THREE

Poet under Tree

AFTER THAT FIRST MEETING with Morgan, Miss Renshaw began to take them to the Ena Thompson Memorial Gardens quite often, at least once a week, sometimes twice. Usually she would tell the little girls to run away and write poems, but other times she made them all sit down in a circle under the fig tree and listen to Morgan.

"Poets know so much," said Miss Renshaw. "You should listen to Morgan; he knows. About nature. About life."

They didn't mind; it was easy to listen to Morgan. Not only his eyes were beautiful, but so was his voice, low and owlish. He talked and talked. He smoked while he spoke, and his cigarettes had a strong smell, like burnt Christmas pudding. Morgan knew all about flowers and plants and soil and earth. He knew how living things catch life and grow, and then how death arrives and they lie down and give up.

"But I don't let them give up," said Morgan. "I make them feel powerful again, so that they can keep going."

Morgan was tender; he held the dying plants gently in his hands, the same hands that took up a pen with ink as brown as the earth and wrote his poems in the black leather book he kept in his top pocket, like a miniature Bible. When he had finished mowing the lawn or planting bulbs or digging up weeds, he would sit under the tree, and thoughts of poems would come to him as he smoked. Words entered his mind through the thin violet beauty of the smoke winding upward to the sky, and down he would write them until it was time to get up and start digging again.

Morgan knew more about the secrets of the earth than anyone alive.

"From his childhood, Morgan has belonged to the earth," Miss Renshaw told them.

Well, he likes digging, thought Cubby. Morgan had a giant shovel that he would send sharply into the chocolate earth like an ax.

"Morgan is a conscientious objector," said Miss Renshaw. "Do you know what that is?"

Nobody dared answer. Sometimes Miss Renshaw did not want an answer; she wanted another question.

"What is it, Miss Renshaw?" asked Bethany at last.

"A conscientious objector is a person who refuses to fight

in war, refuses to join the army, even when conscripted. Surely you little girls must know what conscription is?" said Miss Renshaw, her voice rising in despair.

In the distance, past the seawall, they could hear the cries of seagulls and the lapping of the ocean, and they breathed in gusts of salty air. Beyond, they knew there was war, far, far away somewhere else, in Vietnam. That's what conscription was for. Boys left school and got into uniforms and went on boats and planes to fight in the war. Boys and men, off they went.

But not all of them. Not Morgan. Morgan knew it was bad to kill people, to run through a village with a gun and scream and shout and throw bombs at children and mothers. Morgan would not join the army. Instead he tended the Ena Thompson Memorial Gardens and composed poems in his little leather book.

"We won't mention these meetings with Morgan to our parents or other staff, will we, girls?" said Miss Renshaw when they were safely back in the classroom, their round straw hats hung on the pegs on the wall like a row of faded moons. "We won't mention Morgan. Will we?"

"Why not, Miss Renshaw?" asked Bethany.

Miss Renshaw breathed in and out, deeply. Miss Renshaw was good at breathing. She had learned to breathe properly because she had trained to be an actress, and actresses need to breathe very deeply so they can say all their words long and loud. She tried to make the girls breathe deeply too. "Breathe down," Miss Renshaw would say. "Not in, down — into the diaphragm. Feel your diaphragm. Can you feel it?" But none of them could, although Cynthia thought she might have once.

Why not, Miss Renshaw? asked eleven pairs of eyes, and Miss Renshaw breathed deeply and did not answer. Not exactly, anyway.

"I know I can trust you, girls," said Miss Renshaw. "It will be our little secret."

Out in the playground, the little girls sat on wooden benches and ate their sandwiches and played with one another's hair.

"Miss Renshaw loves Morgan," said Georgina. "I saw them kissing."

"No, you didn't," said one of the Elizabeths at once. "That's disgusting."

"Where did you see them?" asked Martine, naturally curious.

Georgina wouldn't say. She turned red. She had freckles, lots and lots and lots of them, and when she blushed, it looked as though there were even more.

Where did Morgan live? Cubby wondered. Did he have a house with rooms, like other people? Or did he live in the gardens, sheltered by the trees, nestling between the massive armlike roots at night when the gates of the gardens were locked shut and nobody could get in or out. Only Morgan remained, trapped inside like the little insect in the teardrop of amber that hung around Miss Renshaw's neck.

"This little creature fell in honey hundreds of thousands of years ago," said Miss Renshaw, holding up her necklace to show them. "Think of that, girls. It's been there ever since."

The sunlight glinted through the golden drop, revealing a net of tiny limbs and wings.

"Oh, Miss Renshaw," said Bethany, aghast, her eyes filling with tears. "The poor thing."

"Now, now, Bethany," said Miss Renshaw briskly. "We can't be crying for every dead creature on earth. It's not reasonable. Save your tears for greater sorrows, girls."

Probably Miss Renshaw was right, thought Cubby. Certainly the sorrow she felt for the insect in the golden necklace was nothing compared to the dropping of her stomach when she had found her pet guinea pig, Agamemnon, dead in his cage on a very hot day in the summer when it was more than a hundred degrees and birds fell from the sky in the South Australian desert.

> *"A shudder in the loins engenders there*
> *The broken wall, the burning roof and tower*
> *And Agamemnon dead!"*

Miss Renshaw cried out unexpectedly, reading aloud from her favorite collection of poetry. She stood by the window looking noble, and her voice had a thickness in it, almost as though she might be about to cry. The windows were high and webbed, edged with cracking paint.

Of course, that poem was about another Agamemnon altogether, not a poor guinea pig lying on his back with his little legs stiffly in the air and his fur all spiky, almost as though he had fallen from the sky himself. "Save your tears for greater sorrows," Miss Renshaw had said, but then, reflected Cubby, Miss Renshaw hadn't known Agamemnon.

FOUR

Four Schoolgirls

"ICARA! CUBBY! STAY TOGETHER!"

On the morning Ronald Ryan was hanged, the voice of Miss Renshaw sailed across the treetops as the little girls dispersed like drops of light rain, down the winding paths and through the maze of shrubs and flower beds. Cubby would certainly have stayed with Icara, but she couldn't see her anywhere. How still it was! A white cat sat by itself on a painted bench, its tail twisting. When it saw Cubby, it leaped from the bench onto the bright-green carpet of grass and ran into the wet labyrinth of the trees.

"Cubby!"

She turned. Martine and Bethany were galloping toward her from the other side of the pond, two little girls in identical hats with bunches of hair bouncing out from underneath. Martine was new to the school. She was from New Caledonia, so she spoke English with a French accent. Her parents had brought her to Sydney to go to school because they said she was learning nothing at all in New Caledonia. Nothing!

"But you can speak French," said Cubby. This was miraculous to the little girls. "We can't speak anything."

"You can speak English," Martine pointed out.

Oh, English. Anyone could speak English.

Martine came from New Caledonia on a big white boat covered with fairy lights.

"There was a swimming pool on board," she told them, "and every night you could have as much ice cream as you wanted. But my brother was seasick and he couldn't eat any of it at all."

"Did you get seasick?" asked Cubby.

"Not once," said Martine with satisfaction.

Martine was very neat. She sat down on the grass, careful not to crease the skirt of her tunic. Her long white socks had frills on top. She had brought them all the way from New Caledonia. Bethany flopped face forward next to her.

The golden February sun glowed high above their heads, and the ducks swam to and fro on the pond. Cubby sank to the ground and lay on her back with her eyes wide open.

"Look," said Martine from her sitting-up position. "There's Icara."

Cubby raised her head. Icara was walking toward them, scuffing her shoes on the path, both her arms loosely swinging. Humming, she sat down on the grass next to the others.

The sun lay upon their shoulders like a summer blanket. They breathed in the warm air and the scent of flowers and listened to the sounds of unseen animals rustling in the reedy islands of the pond. A little breeze rose from the harbor.

"I wonder who Ena Thompson was," said Bethany, getting up on her elbow. "To have a whole park named after her."

"She must have been famous," said Cubby.

"But what could she have been famous for?"

"Swimming," suggested Martine. "Maybe she swam to New Zealand."

They thought about it.

"New Zealand is too far," said Icara. "Nobody could swim that far."

("Icara is a realist," Miss Renshaw had said, "but the world needs dreamers, not realists.")

New Zealand, Nouméa, the Cook Islands, Hawaii, Cubby thought sleepily. She looked up at the sky, which was like a great big ocean, with drifts of clouds as islands. On the blackboard Miss Renshaw had drawn a wonderful chalk map of the South Seas, with a curling line of pink dashes to show where Captain Cook had sailed, right to the very end.

"Maybe Ena Thompson died here, in the park," said Bethany, rolling over on her side. The realization of this thought spread in shock over her whole face. "Maybe she fell out of a tree and died, and then her husband buried her under it."

"Maybe she was stung to death by a bee," said Martine. She had once been stung by a bee in the Ena Thompson Memorial Gardens, although it had not led to death. "I hate bees."

"Maybe there's a ghost," said Bethany. "The ghost of Ena Thompson."

Could you have a ghost outside, in a garden? Cubby had always thought that ghosts were only found in houses, creeping up stairways, hiding in cupboards.

"There's no such thing as ghosts," said Icara.

"Yes, there is," said Martine. "I've seen one."

Bethany sat up straight.

"Where?"

"At home," said Martine, in a matter-of-fact way. "On the Isle of Pines."

"The Isle of Pines! Tell us, tell us, tell us." They bent toward her. "Tell us."

"It was my grandmother," said Martine, pleased with the attention. "She was dead for three years already, but I saw her. It was at night. She went into my father's bedroom, where he was sleeping. I crept in and watched."

"What happened?"

"Nothing happened. She just lay there on the bed next to him," said Martine, "like a cat."

That was it?

"Then what happened?"

"Then she just got up and went away."

"Did she walk through the wall?"

Martine shook her head. She was bored with the story now.

"I don't remember. She just wasn't there anymore." She straightened up the frills on her socks. "It was not so special. Everyone sees ghosts on the Isle of Pines. It's normal."

Normal?

"It was just your imagination," said Cubby, looking at Icara, hoping. "Wasn't it?"

"I don't have any imagination," Martine pointed out smugly. "Miss Renshaw said so."

The four girls were sick of sitting. Shifting like spoonfuls of sticky toffee, they got up from the grass. They drifted together toward the duck pond and stood with their arms resting on the railing, watching the duck families swimming forward and backward. The black water swirled below them.

Maybe there are ghosts, thought Cubby. *Maybe they're like the feet of the ducks. They're there underneath, there in the dark, and we just can't see them. . . .*

"Let's go and find Miss Renshaw," said Bethany.

They made their way up one of the several winding paths, half slipping on the leaves underfoot, through the overhanging trees that were heavy with the smell of drowsy fruit bats. It didn't take them long. Miss Renshaw and the other seven little girls were sitting with Morgan, cross-legged in a circle under the fig tree. When Miss Renshaw saw them, she waved. She seemed excited.

"Girls! Where have you been? We've been looking for you. Sit down, quickly and quietly. Q and Q."

Cubby, Icara, Martine, and Bethany squeezed themselves into the circle. Morgan rubbed his beard and smiled, but seriously.

"Welcome," he said in his owl's voice.

"Morgan is going to take us somewhere special today, girls," said Miss Renshaw. "You are very lucky."

"Ouch!" said Bethany loudly. Then she whispered, "Sorry, an ant bit me."

Miss Renshaw frowned.

"This is a sad day, as you know, girls," she reminded them. "A very sad day."

The little girls tried to remember the sad day. That's right. Ronald Ryan. But already thoughts of Ronald Ryan had flown away like feathers.

"So that's why we are going to do something very special," Miss Renshaw went on, "to help us remember this sad day. Now, listen to Morgan."

Listen to Morgan, listen to Morgan. It was easy to listen to Morgan and his deep, bubbling words and his wispy hair floating over his eyes. . . .

"There are many secret places," Morgan said, looking around the circle, but somehow not really looking at them. "So many hidden spots along the harbor, places nobody knows about."

"You know about them," said Georgina.

"It's just a way of speaking, Georgina," said Miss Renshaw, irritated. "Don't interrupt."

"Places hardly anyone knows about," Morgan corrected himself.

Caves, he said, hidden caves with Aboriginal paintings from the Dreamtime, thousands of years old, he said.

"We know about the Dreamtime," said the tallest Elizabeth.

"Last year in Term One we did fairy tales, in Term Two we did Greek myths, and in Term Three we did the Dreamtime." She counted them off with her fingers.

"I hate myths," said Martine.

"Ah, but you don't really know about the Dreamtime," said Morgan, pulling a cigarette from his top pocket, "if you haven't seen these caves."

"Are you an Aborigine?" asked Cynthia.

An Aborigine! The little girls had never met an Aborigine. But no. Morgan tapped the cigarette on the back of his hand. No, he said, no, he wasn't, but as a child he had spent time with a tribe and they had taught him many things.

"Where did the tribe live?" asked Icara.

"In the outback," said Morgan.

"Where in the outback?" persisted Icara.

Miss Renshaw was annoyed.

"Don't interrupt, Icara," she said sharply. "Allow Morgan to finish what he was telling you."

Don't interrupt, don't interrupt, listen to Morgan. Morgan is a special person; you girls are lucky to know him.

"You are extremely lucky today," said Miss Renshaw, not allowing Morgan to finish what he was saying, "because Morgan is going to take us to one of these hidden caves."

The little girls stared.

"They are in a very secret place, but he will lead us there. A secret place. We will be privileged to see some ancient sacred paintings from the Dreamtime."

They sat as silent as snails.

"I think I can trust you, each one of you." Miss Renshaw paused. "I hope you understand."

It's our little secret, isn't it, girls?

"Now?" asked Bethany, her eyes large, large, larger.

"Right now," said Morgan, standing up in his big work boots and his straw hat. He put the cigarette in his mouth and took out a lighter from his pocket.

"Come along, girls," said Miss Renshaw, crisp and eager, getting up and brushing the grass from the skirt of her dress. "On your feet."

"I don't want to go, Miss Renshaw," said Bethany.

Miss Renshaw paid no attention. After all, Bethany never wanted to go anywhere.

"I'm scared of caves," pleaded Bethany. "Please, can I stay behind?"

"Don't be silly, Bethany," Miss Renshaw replied. "Nobody is staying behind. Come on, on your feet and follow Morgan."

"Are you a hippie, Morgan?" the tallest Elizabeth asked him as she stood up, shaking her legs to get rid of the pins and needles.

"Hippies are only in America," said Cynthia.

"No, they're not," retorted Elizabeth. "Remember, we saw some in Hyde Park."

It was true: they had seen hippies in Hyde Park when Miss Renshaw took them into town to the Australian Museum. A group of people were lying on blankets, with hair as long as Rapunzel's and dresses down to their feet, even the men, and they had no shoes and played guitars and tambourines, and they were selling strings of multicolored beads and necklaces made out of watermelon seeds.

But Morgan had not heard the question. Already he was striding ahead toward the water, like the cat with the seven-league boots.

"Come along, quickly now, girls," cried Miss Renshaw. "There's nothing to be afraid of. Nothing at all."

The sky, which had seemed so vastly blue a moment before, now had mysteriously clouded over, and the air had a purple light, like dying lavender on a hot, hot day. Even the air seemed to smell of lavender to Cubby, like the very old ladies that sat in the back of the church with their walking sticks and their black velvet bags.

She looked over at Bethany, at her little face, pale and creased. And quite suddenly, Cubby did feel afraid.

FIVE

Schoolgirl and Shadow

IT WAS NOT POSSIBLE TO SAY NO, in any case. "We must all work together for the common good," as Miss Renshaw would say. So the eleven little girls, half reluctant and half eager, including Bethany, followed Morgan along the pathway toward the shore, beyond the edges of the Ena Thompson Memorial Gardens.

"I hope this isn't going to take hours," said Georgina. "We'd better be back in time for snack."

They all knew what she meant. Every snack time Georgina had a pineapple doughnut that her mother had bought at the pastry shop and which she ate in great gulps like a dog.

"Boo-hoo," said Elizabeth with the plaits, who never had anything good for snack.

"My feet hurt," said Martine. Her shoes were also from New Caledonia. They were shiny and pretty like ballet slippers and had silver buckles instead of laces.

Ahead of them they could see Morgan climbing down the sandstone wall encrusted with mussel shells that separated the gardens from the Pacific Ocean. They watched him turn and hold out his hand for Miss Renshaw, and then she, too, leaped down from the wall. He gestured at them from a distance, his long arms making loops in the air.

"I guess the cave must be down there," said the tallest Elizabeth. "We have to get down on the beach."

"Oh, do we have to?" Bethany wailed, but now in her voice was an edge of pleasure.

32

They had never done anything like this before — get down onto the beach! What if somebody saw them? *Remember, girls, you are representing the school.* Now instead of dawdling, they broke into a run to see who could be there first.

They waited in turn above the wall while Morgan helped them down. One by one they each took his hand, that tender, dusty hand that nurtured dying plants back to life, and jumped, one by one, down onto the beach. It was hardly a beach, more a rocky platform. The waves lapped forward over shelves of rocks and filled the empty craters with water. Inside the rock pools there were shells and crabs and even tiny silver fish.

"You've got to watch it here," warned Morgan. "Keep your balance. The rocks are slippery. We don't want anyone breaking a leg."

"What did he say?" asked Bethany, jumping, and then she

slipped and screamed so loudly that for a moment Cubby thought she must have died, although then she remembered that if Bethany had died, she couldn't have screamed.

Bethany wasn't dead, but her knee was badly scraped and there was blood everywhere and tears came pouring out of her blue eyes.

"Oh, dear, Bethany, goodness me, you silly girl," said Miss Renshaw, shaking her head, exasperated. "You really must listen to what you're told."

"I couldn't hear," began Bethany in a blubber, but then Morgan splashed water gently over the wound, so the blood flowed off into the ocean, never to be seen again. He pulled her sock right up over her knee.

"Are you all right to walk?" he asked, and Bethany sniffed, so Morgan lifted her up and slung her over his back like a mother koala. "Piggyback time," he said.

Bethany grinned backward at the others through the remains of tears, triumphantly.

"It's because she's so small," muttered tall Elizabeth. "I bet he wouldn't have carried me."

"Stop talking, Elizabeth," said Miss Renshaw, "and concentrate on walking."

They picked their way painstakingly along the rocky coast, which slowly began to become sand. The waves crept up and soaked their black school shoes, their socks, and Miss Renshaw's shoes and stockings. The sun grew strong behind gathering gray clouds and burned their eyes.

They turned a corner of the coastline and came face-to-face with a man standing on the shore, drying himself with a towel. He had obviously just been swimming, and he was completely naked. The naked man gazed at them, monumental and whalelike.

The little girls were shocked to the core.

"Is this a nudist beach?" Cynthia asked Miss Renshaw, trying not to laugh.

But Miss Renshaw, her head bent down, quickened her pace. They stumbled after her, half looking back and half looking away.

They turned another bend, and the naked man was gone. Then it was windy, so windy that Martine's hat blew off. They watched it rise up in the air and then out, gathering speed, around and around like the wheel of a car, until it landed in the waves. It bobbed there, a little circular boat of straw.

"Oh, dear," said Miss Renshaw, grimacing. "We don't want to lose any more. Girls, you must hang on to your hats."

"I don't care," said Martine, tossing her head. "I hate that hat."

"Your mother will not be pleased," said Miss Renshaw, "whatever you may think of it. Everything costs money."

"We're nearly there," said Morgan.

He let Bethany gently down from his back. Blood oozed from her knee through the white sock.

"Thank you, Morgan," said Bethany, sniffing.

They straggled after Morgan, up to where he stood in front of an opening in the cliff face. It was like a huge mouth.

"This is it," said Morgan. "This is where we get in."

This was it? This was the cave? But it was so low.

"You're all going to have to bend down as much as you can at the beginning," said Morgan, "so you don't bang your heads."

"I don't want to go in," said Bethany.

"It's just at the beginning that it's like this," said Morgan. "There's a narrow passageway just for a few yards, then it opens out and you can stand up straight."

"Leave your hats outside, girls," said Miss Renshaw. Her eyes were bright with excitement, and the amber bead around her neck glowed. "Fill them with sand, so they don't blow away."

"I don't want to go in," said Bethany.

But she joined the others as they piled their hats into a little tower and threw sand over them to weigh them down.

"Remember, girls," said Miss Renshaw. "No silliness. This is going to be a very special experience."

"Like that nude man," whispered Georgina, swallowing her laugh.

"I don't want to go in," said Bethany.

Morgan lowered his head and squeezed into the cave's entrance. Miss Renshaw went after him, pulling in her springy hair. The little girls bent their knees and started to make their way through the opening. What else could they do? Cubby knelt, quaking, behind Icara. She didn't want to go into this deep, black, wet cave any more than Bethany did. But they couldn't stay outside. Miss Renshaw wouldn't let them. So she followed the others, feeling the rocks with her hands and under her feet, into the darkness.

The roof of the cave swung down over them, and the walls closed in and the light of day disappeared.

"Something smells funny," said Cynthia.

There was an ancient, dripping sound, as though water had been raining down for centuries.

"But it's not a bad smell," said the short Elizabeth.

It wasn't dark for long. Morgan had a flashlight. He took it from his pocket, switched it on, and shone it briefly over their faces. Martine made a squeak of laughter.

"Shhh!" said Miss Renshaw.

"Sorry," murmured Martine.

"She's got the giggles," said Georgina unnecessarily.

"I can't breathe!" said Elizabeth with the plaits. "There's no air in here."

"Take it easy," said Morgan. "There's plenty of air for everyone."

They shuffled forward, like segments of a caterpillar. On the wall beside them, their shadows grew in the flashlight beam. Bethany, whose fear had gone as quickly as it came, held up her tiny hand, and it was huge.

"Look! I'm a giant!"

"Shhhhhh."

The tunnel had opened up into a wider space. They could stand up now, just as Morgan had promised. But it was so dark. *As dark as death,* Cubby thought.

"Oh!"

Morgan shone his flashlight on the roof and walls of the old, old cave. The little girls felt wrapped up in a strange silence.

It was as though outside the birds had stopped singing and the waves had stopped rolling and the leaves of the trees had stopped shaking and falling in the wind.

"Look," said Morgan.

The light swung up and down the rocky wall, like a swooping bird with wings made of light.

"Thousands of years old," said Miss Renshaw softly. "Thousands and thousands of years. Think of that, girls. These paintings have been here all those thousands of years. There were people here, inside this cave."

Cubby stared at the wall of shaking light. She had imagined big drawings of kangaroos or people with spears. But she couldn't see anything. Was that something faint and figure-like in the depths of the stone? The flashlight moved away again before she could be sure.

"There!" The light hovered like a spaceship. "And there!"

Cubby had such a feeling of loneliness, even though she could feel the warm breath of the others around her.

It's as though everyone's gone, she thought. *They've all gone, and I'm the only one left.*

Even Icara was gone. Cubby was alone in the cave beyond the realms of the Ena Thompson Memorial Gardens. What were the gardens, after all? Perhaps there were no gardens — there was nothing but a wide, weightless plain of terrible light and freedom, cliffs, and wild trees that nobody had planted but that grew by themselves out of the insides of the earth, to be cut down and turned into the floorboards outside the headmistress's office, that shone like deep ice and were just as cold.

And then she remembered Ronald Ryan, and how he had been hanged that morning, the rope around his neck and the hood over his face and his feet stepping out into an empty space. . . .

"Miss Renshaw, can we leave now?" she heard someone say. "It's my asthma."

"Can we go, Miss Renshaw? Can we go? Can we go?"

Eleven little girls, pressed up against one another, breathing, squeaking, fidgeting.

But "Wait, girls," breathed Miss Renshaw. "Wait. Not now."

SIX

Hide and Seek

"Wait," Miss Renshaw had said. "Not now."

But they didn't wait. It was Cynthia who couldn't wait, wheezing, gasping for breath, who went first, and then the others after her. Miss Renshaw didn't call out to them, *Stop girls, stop at once.* So they didn't stop. They stumbled along in a line, back the way they had come, crawling out through the low tunnel, back to the cave's mouth, back outside, back into the world they knew. There was no light to guide them, as Morgan had turned his flashlight off and they couldn't see anything, so they had to lead themselves.

They came out into the sunshine and the wind, one after the other like dice falling from a cup. There was their pile of hats, just as they had left them. The little girls picked them up, shaking off the sand.

"Am I glad to be out of there," said Bethany.

The sun shone down on them in great wide beams. The little girls sat on the rocks and the sand and the tufts of sea grass and waited for Morgan and Miss Renshaw. Bethany inspected her wounded knee. Martine stretched out to sunbathe her tanned legs, pulling up the skirt of her uniform as far as she could.

Elizabeth the taller and Elizabeth the shorter began to sing a hand-slapping game:

"Under the bamboo
Under the tree
True loves forever
True loves we'll be.
And when we're married
We'll raise a family
Under the shady
Bamboo tree."

"When's Miss Renshaw coming?" complained Georgina with a yawn. "She's taking ages."

"She didn't want to come out," said Bethany. "She liked it in there."

"Maybe he's showing her another painting," said Elizabeth with the plaits.

"Maybe he's kissing her," said Cynthia.

The little girls, even silent Deirdre, collapsed in laughter.

"I want to go," said Georgina, thinking of her pineapple doughnut.

They were all hungry, and their feet were wet. But they waited. They had to wait for their teacher.

"Oh!" cried Martine, suddenly jumping up in her frilled socks, pointing. "Look! It's my hat!"

Out on the surface of the waves, only a few yards from the beach, sat Martine's hat. It hadn't been carried off to South America or the Antarctic but had been blown back to shore. Now it was bobbing there, not too far out, like a little duck waiting trustingly for its mother.

"I'll get it!" said Georgina, who had already pulled off her shoes and socks.

They danced up and down on the shore, watching Georgina step out into the ocean to rescue the runaway hat.

"It's freezing!" screeched Georgina, reaching forward, nearly falling in.

The waves came up to her thighs, and the hem of her uniform was soaked. She grasped the hat, then staggered back to land, holding it out to Martine.

"It's so wet," said Martine. She pulled it on her head.

"You look like a scarecrow," said the oldest Elizabeth.

"I hate this hat anyway," said Martine.

"Well, thanks for saying thanks," muttered Georgina.

"Oh, thanks, then," retorted Martine.

They waited. But Miss Renshaw did not come.

"I'm so hungry," wailed Georgina as she put her shoes and socks back on. "I'm starving to death."

Icara climbed up onto the top of a high, smooth sandstone boulder and sat with her arms wrapped around her knees, like a listless monkey. Cubby kept looking for Miss Renshaw — it was like waiting for a bus, constantly thinking that each little sound was Miss Renshaw and Morgan coming back.

Bethany stood at where they had entered the cave and cupped her hands around her mouth.

"Miss Renshaw!" she yelled. "Miss Renshaw!"

There was no answer, not even an echo.

"Should we go back in and find her?" suggested Cynthia.

But none of them wanted to go into that darkness again.

"Maybe they went out another way," said the tallest Elizabeth.

That was possible. After all, didn't Morgan know more about the seashore than anyone alive? There might be any number of ways back out of the cave.

"The tide's coming in," observed Icara from her place on the rock.

"Maybe if we went back to the gardens," said Cubby tentatively, "and waited for them there."

Nobody agreed, and nobody disagreed. But the tide was coming in, and they couldn't stay where they were. Soon the bay would be filled with waves, and there would be nowhere left to stand. So without making a particular decision, the little girls began to step back along the rocky edge of the world, without their teacher.

They met no one on the way. The swimmer they had surprised on their journey to the cave was no longer there.

"That's a relief," said Georgina.

They pulled themselves up the sandstone wall, one by one, back into the protection of the Ena Thompson Memorial Gardens. Now there were other people about—a man in a suit, walking briskly; a pair of women in hats; a mother pushing a pram with a child beside her; a very old man sitting on a bench reading a newspaper. But there was no Miss Renshaw.

"And no Morgan," said Cynthia.

> *"Captain Cook*
> *Chased a chook*
> *All around Australia;*
> *Lost his pants*
> *In the middle of France*
> *And found them in Tasmania,"*

sang the two Elizabeths.

"She must have gotten out another way," said Bethany.

"Could she have gone back to school already?" said Elizabeth with the plaits.

Without us? The little girls looked at one another. Blue, green, black, brown, gray eyes. Hazel eyes flecked with yellow.

"I suppose we could ask people," said Georgina doubtfully, "if they've seen her."

But nobody wanted to ask. What would they say?

"Let's look for her," said Cynthia.

How they looked! They looked behind bushes and up trees. They hunted for Miss Renshaw in the Glade of Roses and the

Grove of Succulents, around the Wishing Tree and through the Fairy Bower and the Tropical Greenhouse. They went into the toilet block and looked in every gloomy cubicle. They even went to the shed where Morgan kept his tools, but the corrugated-iron door was locked up with a large rusty padlock. Bethany banged on the door.

"Miss Renshaw!" she called out, just as she had at the mouth of the cave. "Miss Renshaw!"

"She wouldn't be in there," said Martine.

No, she wouldn't be in there, that dark, dirty place, squeezed up with lawn mowers and rubber hoses and rows of shovels. But where would she be? All the time they were expecting to see her, coming up the path in her droopy crimson dress or sitting with Morgan under a tree as he smoked a cigarette or wrote a line of poetry in his little leather book. But she was nowhere.

"She must have gone back to school," said Elizabeth with the plaits decisively.

"We're going to get in trouble!" Bethany put her hands to her face and began to sob.

The other girls paid no attention. They were used to Bethany breaking down in tears. Why, she had cried nonstop for two weeks when she came second to last in a mental arithmetic test.

"Should we go back to school by ourselves?" asked Martine. "I mean, what else can we do?"

The little girls considered.

"Anything we do will be wrong," said silent Deirdre dolefully, speaking at last.

That was true enough. Yet what else could they do but go back? They couldn't wait here forever.

"I'm hungry," said Georgina, because she still hoped to be there in time for her pineapple doughnut.

SEVEN

Schoolgirl Crying

BUT SNACK TIME WAS LONG OVER by the time they got back to school. They slunk through the yellow gate into the silent playground. Trembling, they tiptoed, all eleven of them, up the four flights of sticky stairs, their little hearts beating inside their little chests, *bumpety-bumpety,* like eleven tin monkeys banging on drums. Up, up, up, past the closed doors of the chapel, past the office of the deputy headmistress, past the teachers' staff room, right up to the very top of the school, in through the door of their classroom.

Perhaps they hoped Miss Renshaw would be standing impatiently in front of the blackboard, a stick of chalk in her hand. *Where have you been, you silly girls? Never do that again. I expect more of you. Remember, you are representing the school.*

But Miss Renshaw was not there. The classroom was empty, just the wind coming through the high, half-open window. They filed in and scattered around, opening bags, finding bits of food in their lunch boxes — packets of raisins, bananas, crackers with Vegemite.

Bethany, whose tears had dried during the walk back, began to cry again. Elizabeth with the plaits sighed and gave in. She walked over to the crouching Bethany and put an arm around her.

"Do you want to go to see Matron?"

No, no, no. Bethany shook her head vehemently, sobbing even louder. Not Matron! Matron stalked the corridors of the school, accompanied by two overweight, aging dachshunds with grizzled jaws and filthy tempers. Bethany had not yet come to that.

"Girls!"

The door of the classroom swung open. They had been so preoccupied they'd not heard the sound of the approaching footsteps.

"What is going on here? What is all this noise?" demanded a piercing voice of disapproval over the pushing back of chairs and shuffling of feet as the eleven little girls, even weeping Bethany, stood up, the way they had been taught to do when any adult entered the room.

It was Dr. Strangemeadows. She taught French to the higher classes. The little girls only knew her by sight. She had a huge head of black hair in a bun and wonderfully impressive eyelashes. When she spoke, she was like a Roman emperor.

"Why are you alone in the classroom?" demanded Dr. Strangemeadows. "I saw you all through my window, tramping up here like stray puppies. Where is your teacher?"

Nobody spoke. They stood, waiting. Always waiting. Dr. Strangemeadows frowned.

"Who is your teacher? Who should be here with you now?"

At least this they could answer.

"Miss Renshaw," they said severally, all about the room.

"Miss Renshaw," repeated Dr. Strangemeadows. "Well, then, where is Miss Renshaw? Do stop sniffing," she said, looking at Bethany with a pained expression. "And use a hankie, please.

Have you got a hankie?"

Bethany hid her face in the elbow of her uniform. Apart from her snuffles, nobody made a sound.

"Oh, for heaven's sake, girls," snapped Dr. Strangemeadows. "Don't waste my time. I have a class to teach. Where is Miss Renshaw?"

"We lost her!" burst out Bethany, her voice muffled by navy blue, but loud enough.

Someone moved their seat; there was a screech on the linoleum floor.

"Lost her?" repeated Dr. Strangemeadows. "What on earth do you mean, lost her?"

The little girls did not know how to explain. They didn't know where to begin. Or where to end.

"We went to the park," attempted Georgina. "To the gardens."

Dr. Strangemeadows turned her noble head to Georgina.

"You lost Miss Renshaw in the gardens?"

Georgina nodded. She licked her lips.

"Not just me," she added quickly. "All of us."

"So you came back to school without her?" Dr. Strange-meadows seemed relieved. "Really, girls, how ridiculous. Whatever possessed you? Miss Renshaw will be down there in the gardens, out of her mind, looking for you!"

She tapped on Deirdre's desk, which was right at the front.

"Have you got some work to get on with? Don't answer me no, because I know you have. What work have you to get on with?"

Deirdre pulled out a book.

"Wr-wr-writing," she stammered.

She held it up, but Dr. Strangemeadows was supremely uninterested.

"Very well. Writing. Sit down, girls, and get out your writing books and continue with whatever work you have been doing with Miss Renshaw. And"—she raised a hand in the air—"do not waste my time telling me she has given you nothing to get on with, because I know that to be absolutely untrue. I expect each one of you to work hard, without making any noise, while I go and see what on earth has happened."

She was gone, instantaneously, like an apparition.

"We're in big trouble," said Cynthia.

Nobody answered. Shocked into obedience, the little girls pulled out their writing books and picked up their pencils and began filling in the blanks between the words on the page.

Subject, Predicate, Noun. These were things to cool their panic. Finite Verbs, Adverbial Clauses, Adjectival Phrases. These things were eternal — they could not change or disappear, like Miss Renshaw. The little girls filled in the spaces and they waited. Something would happen, they knew, very soon.

And it did. The next person to arrive, within minutes, if not moments, was the deputy headmistress, Mrs. Arnold. Again, they sprang up like jack-in-the-boxes as she came in the door.

"Sit down, sit down, girls, please," said Mrs. Arnold.

Mrs. Arnold was thin and gray and her back was bent, and she oozed cigarette smoke. Her hands shook as she spoke, and she often stopped to cough and catch her breath. But her eyes, under the black-rimmed glasses and deep in the wrinkled face, were invariably kind.

"Now, let me say first, nobody is in trouble," said Mrs. Arnold.

They did not believe her. They couldn't. They knew they were in trouble, very big trouble. They had lost their teacher!

"I just need to get a few facts straight," said Mrs. Arnold, sitting herself on Miss Renshaw's cluttered desk, making a space by pushing back a pile of papers and a tin of colored pencils. "I've just been speaking with Dr. Strangemeadows. Let me understand. We seem to be missing Miss Renshaw, is that right?"

They nodded.

"So let's just take this step-by-step. Miss Renshaw took you down to the Ena Thompson Gardens this morning. For a lesson of some sort, is that right?"

They were silent.

Then Georgina muttered, "To think about death."

Mrs. Arnold leaned forward with her good ear.

"What was that?"

Elizabeth with the plaits intervened in a louder voice: "To write poems."

Mrs. Arnold coughed and spluttered.

"Very good, very good, to write poems."

"Yes," said the little girls.

"So down you went. So you sat in the gardens together, and what — talked about what you were seeing, hearing, smelling? To write poems, these are the sorts of things you need to think about, aren't they?"

They nodded.

"Have you written poems, Mrs. Arnold?" asked Bethany, wiping tears from her cheeks.

Mrs. Arnold was not to be diverted.

"So, there you all are, writing poems. And at some stage, I take it, you were separated from Miss Renshaw? She went somewhere?"

Silence.

"To get a drink? Something like that?"

Silence.

"You see, girls, I can't understand how you became parted. You were in the gardens with your teacher. How is it that you lost sight of each other? How is it that you've come back to school without her? This is the part I simply cannot understand."

She broke into more coughs. She put a hand on the desk to

steady herself. Some papers fluttered to the floor, settling like soft birds.

The cave. The cave. Morgan. The cave.

We won't mention this, will we, girls? We won't mention this to anyone. It will be our secret.

"Goodness me, we'd better find her, then," said Mrs. Arnold. She straightened up to leave, and the little girls once more all rose to their feet. "Get on with your work, quietly now. Someone will be up shortly to take over until, er, until Miss Renshaw comes back."

"Mrs. Arnold?" Bethany put up her hand. Her face was wet and woebegone.

"Yes?" said Mrs. Arnold, pausing at the door, her hand on the handle.

Bethany tugged on a tear-sodden plait.

"Miss Renshaw will come back, won't she?" she asked.

"Of course she'll come back." Mrs. Arnold broke into a mystified smile. "She'll come back, you silly child. There's no question of that. She's just down at the gardens, looking for you all. Dear me."

And she left, looking down at the ground, shaking her head. They heard her footsteps starting down the stairs.

"We should have told," said Martine, glancing around furtively.

They knew what she meant. They should have told Mrs. Arnold about the cave. About Morgan. Morgan, with his beard and his beautiful eyes, and his sweet-smelling cigarettes.

They should have told.

"Maybe Morgan and Miss Renshaw met someone they knew," said the oldest Elizabeth. "They ran into someone and they all got talking."

"In that cave?" said Icara. "Who are you going to meet in a cave?"

Icara is a realist, but the world needs dreamers, not realists.

"But she will come back?" said Bethany, turning to them all, beseeching, her blue eyes full of translucent tears. "Miss Renshaw will come back?"

"Yes, yes, she'll come back," groaned Georgina, putting the necessary arm around Bethany again. "She's probably coming in the gate right now."

They could almost hear the gate falling open, hinges squeaking. They could almost hear Miss Renshaw coming up the stairs, clicking her heels on the sixty-seven gray-green steps. Almost.

Cubby put down her pencil. She had lost heart somehow. She looked up at the blackboard. Across its flat rectangular expanse stretched the wondrous South Pacific Ocean as drawn by Miss Renshaw, complete with curling blue-chalk waves and a white compass marked North South East West. There was a line of pink dashes showing the path of Captain Cook's boat, the *Endeavour,* like a pink snail trail.

Cubby blinked. Suddenly the sounds of the classroom, the sniffing, the rustling of papers and dropping pencils, faded in her ears. She had that bleak feeling that she'd had in the cave, of being alone. She stared at the blackboard. She felt sick.

Because words were forming there, on the board, right before her eyes. Words grew in the middle of the Pacific Ocean, as though they were being written by an invisible hand, in bright-yellow chalk.

Cubby could see them perfectly. Four clear simple words,

Not now. Not ever.

written in Miss Renshaw's own unmistakable, beautiful handwriting.

EIGHT

Floating Schoolgirl

NOBODY ELSE SAW. The other girls were heads down over their books, writing, murmuring, exchanging pencils. Nobody saw a thing. She, Cubby, was the only one.

That was the moment she began to float. Very deliberately, she turned her eyes away from the board and floated upward, swimming through the air, like a dream. She floated out the classroom window, her hat half flying off her head, high above the laneways and streets. She floated all day while they waited for Miss Renshaw to return.

If Dr. Strangemeadows had indeed gone down to the gardens to find Miss Renshaw half out of her mind with worry, she had returned alone. There was no message from anyone and no further visits from Mrs. Arnold. Instead, Miss de Soto, the music teacher, arrived to supervise them for the rest of the day. She was round and fluffy with plump, powdered cheeks and an armful of spectacular jewelry—large rings and jangling bracelets. Her curved glasses were like the eyes of a bee. She brought her guitar slung over her back.

"Put away your work, girls," said Miss de Soto. She tapped her foot. "Come down to the front and sit near me."

Dutifully, and with relief, they sat together on a square of carpet at Miss de Soto's feet.

"That's right. Up close. I want to hear every voice."

"I saw raindrops on my window—
Joy is like the rain!"

sang Miss de Soto, *plink-a-plink* went the guitar, and the little girls, who knew the tune from their music lessons, sang along with her, although with less conviction. Was joy, after all, so much like the rain, really? But they were happy enough to lie on the floor and stretch out like cats and scratch one another on the back, trying not to think.

"I saw clouds upon a mountain—
Joy is like a cloud."

The whole time, Cubby was floating, far above it all.

When the bell rang for the end of the day, Miss de Soto swiftly took herself and her guitar away, down the stairs back to the music room. The eleven little girls packed up their bags and began to leave. Cubby got up from the floor last of all. She was very careful not to look at the blackboard, not even the briefest glimpse. Where was her bag? Her head was giddy, as though she had been spinning around on a swing. She couldn't feel the ground beneath her; her feet were like sponges.

A voice came from behind her, right inside her ear.

"Cubby."

She turned around. It was Icara.

"What?" said Cubby.

Icara looked at her in a concentrated way.

"Do you want to come over to my house?"

Cubby was astonished. Despite their friendship, she had never been asked to Icara's house before. They were the sort of friends who only knew each other at school, never after school, never on the weekends. Why was Icara asking her now? But Cubby was floating — she would go anywhere, do anything.

"All right," she said.

"Good," said Icara.

They walked down the stairs, their bags banging against each other. The playground was full of shouting, of arms and legs and running feet. The boarders lined up for their afternoon cup of tea and handful of sugary biscuits at a table next to the big old bell, with its long rope, which rang at the beginning and end of each school day. At the yellow gate, prefects stood on duty, checking that everyone's uniform was in order, hats on heads, ties around necks.

"Your socks are falling down," said Amanda-fit-to-be-loved

to Cubby as they passed through, and Cubby automatically bent down to pull them up. Within seconds they fell down again.

"Come on," said Icara, tugging at her sleeve.

Cubby had no idea where Icara lived or how she got home, by train, bus, ferry. Icara didn't speak, so Cubby simply followed her, as light as a soap bubble, onto the bus that left from the bottom of the hill every afternoon, carrying great loads of girls away from the city. They sat together near the front, as the bus passed through a tunnel, past shops and along the bay, deep into suburban streets. At each stop more schoolgirls left, until it was just the two of them. The engine of the bus hummed, the brakes squeaked. Icara stood up and pulled the cord.

"This is my stop," she said.

The bus halted next to a tall, leafy tree, on the corner of two shady roads. Cubby floated after Icara off the bus and down the narrower of the two streets. The houses had high walls and two stories and thick, lovely gardens. *Icara must be rich,* thought Cubby suddenly. *These are rich people's houses.*

They stopped outside a building that looked like a museum, made of caramel sandstone bricks with old-fashioned stained-glass windows. Out front was a fishpond, round and ornate like a stone wedding cake. Icara pushed open the gate.

"Is this your house?" asked Cubby.

"Yep," said Icara.

"It looks so old," said Cubby reverently.

"It was built a hundred and ten years ago," said Icara.

A hundred and ten years . . . Cubby was overawed. She knew that in England there were buildings hundreds and hundreds, even thousands, of years old — and in Egypt! Well. But what were the castles of Europe and the pyramids of Egypt to little Cubby? They were like places in the *Thousand and One Nights,* flickering on movie screens or in black-and-white on the television at night, pages in encyclopedias to be flipped over with one hand. But this house was here, in front of her, a whole hundred and ten years old.

The front door had a huge golden doorknob and shiny lock. Icara opened it with her own key. When it swung forward, Icara threw her schoolbag down just inside, next to a hat stand covered with coats and hats.

"You can leave your bag there," she said.

Cubby laid her bag gingerly next to Icara's. Then Icara kicked off her shoes.

"Mrs. Ellerman says I have to," said Icara, pointing to her white-socked feet. "To keep the floor nice. Since you're a guest, it probably doesn't matter."

But Cubby was glad to slip off her own shoes, to feel the solid floor with her toes. She and Icara slid together in their socks across the wide space of tiled floor that opened out before them. They pretended to ice-skate.

"Who's Mrs. Ellerman?" asked Cubby.

"Oh, she looks after us," said Icara casually. "My mother doesn't live here."

"Oh," said Cubby. Then, timidly, "Where does she live?"

"She lives in Los Angeles," said Icara. "In America."

Los Angeles? This made no sense to Cubby. How could a person's mother live in Los Angeles? Icara's parents must be divorced. Cubby didn't know what to say. She didn't know anybody whose parents were divorced. She looked around at the white walls and the paintings with their elaborate frames, the brass light switches. She felt faint and giddy again. *Not now. Not ever.* She put a hand out on the edge of a chair, to stop herself from tipping over.

"Is anybody home?" she asked desperately.

She was not used to such an empty house. Her own house had her little brother and sister, her mother, the dogs, the television.

"Maybe. Maybe upstairs. I don't know."

They had reached the kitchen now. Icara slid over to the fridge and opened the freezer, taking out two red ice pops. She gave one to Cubby.

"Come outside," she said.

They went through a glass door that led to the backyard. Lawn and flowers, white columns, a swimming pool with a huge net next to it, big enough to catch a giant butterfly. Then there was a stretch of bushes, and below that the river, twisted and brown like a huge, gleaming snake. But Cubby hardly noticed the river or anything else. All she saw was a trampoline — imagine having your own trampoline! She turned to Icara.

"Can we go on it?"

"If you want to," said Icara.

The two girls lay on their backs on the trampoline and sucked on their ice pops. Then, red lipped, they got up and jumped, falling on their stomachs and their knees, backward, frontward, sideways, jumping, jumping, jumping. After a while

Icara stopped and sat on the edge of the trampoline, catching her breath. But Cubby couldn't stop. She kept on jumping, higher and higher, as though she were made of rubber, or something even lighter, a sort of springy sponge. Up in the air she stretched out her arms, and it felt like more than flying — it was like a strange sort of wild sleeping.

"Icky!" came a voice suddenly from above. "Icky! Icky!"

Like God, thought Cubby, startled, only it was a woman's voice. She stopped jumping, quite suddenly. Icara groaned and rubbed her face with her hands.

"That's Mrs. Ellerman," she said. "We'd better go in."

Cubby stood for a moment on the shuddering trampoline. The world came rushing around her. She felt herself falling, down and farther down, landing with a thud. She stopped floating almost as suddenly as she had begun.

She slid off the trampoline. The still ground jarred her feet. She would have much preferred to stay outside for the rest of her life, even forever, but she followed Icara up to the house, through the glass doorway, to meet Mrs. Ellerman.

NINE

The Exchange

BUT IT WASN'T IN FACT MRS. ELLERMAN sitting at the long dining table, smoking and reading the paper. It was Icara's father.

"Hallo, Dad," said Icara.

"Well, hallo there," said Icara's father, smiling upward, ashing his cigarette.

Cubby was taken aback. The judge! This was not what she had imagined — a man in shorts and a striped shirt, with reading glasses on his nose. Whenever she'd pictured Icara's father, she'd seen someone noble in a white wig, dressed in a red silken robe, like a kimono.

"This is Cubby," said Icara, gesturing.

"Hello, Cubby," said the judge.

"Hello," said Cubby.

Why was Icara's father at home at four o'clock in the afternoon, anyway? Surely fathers only came home as the sun was setting, with their black hats and tired faces, taking off their coats, removing their cuff links. It reminded Cubby of the fairy tale of the wild swans that Miss Renshaw had read them, although she had not been listening very closely. Wasn't there something about how the brothers had to get back by twilight or they would change into swans? *Something like that,* thought Cubby, confused. In any case, it was hard to imagine the judge turning into a swan.

"How are you, Icara?" asked the judge.

"Oh, all right," said Icara, looking away.

Say something, said Cubby silently to Icara. *Say something. You have to say something about Miss Renshaw!* But Icara turned her head away and said nothing.

"There you are, Icky! I was calling you."

A short, dark-haired woman bustled into the room, carrying a piece of cloth in her hands.

"This is Mrs. Ellerman," said Icara to Cubby. "You know, I was telling you about her."

"Hello," said Cubby. "I'm Cubby."

"Hello! Cubby dear!" Mrs. Ellerman beamed at her with disconcerting pleasure. Cubby was not used to adults being so pleased to see her. "How lovely to meet you. Now, Cubby, I want your opinion, seeing you're here. What do you think of this?"

She held up the piece of cloth. Across it was sewn a whole picture made out of colored threads, a mass of yellow and red flowers surrounded by leaves in several different shades of green.

"Mrs. Ellerman does embroidery," explained Icara.

"They're desert peas," said Mrs. Ellerman, pointing at the flowers. "What do you think?"

"It's beautiful," said Cubby, genuinely amazed.

"I like my sewing," said Mrs. Ellerman, nodding in satisfaction as she folded up the cloth. "Keeps my mind busy."

"Busy, busy, Mrs. Ellerman," said the judge, ashing his cigarette again. "Always so busy."

"That's me, all right," agreed Mrs. Ellerman amiably. "I love my chores. I'd be lost without them, Cubby dear, you know"—and she patted Cubby's shoulder—"picking up the dry cleaning, dropping into the butcher, getting my hair done. Or finding a blue embroidery thread, just a particular shade of azure—you know what I mean, Cubby," said Mrs. Ellerman, twinkling at her like Santa Claus.

The judge stood up from the table. He smiled again at Cubby and touched Icara gently on the arm. Then he took himself up the carpeted staircase, almost stealthily, like a fox Cubby had seen one night through her bedroom window, slinking into the bushes.

"How was school, then?" asked Mrs. Ellerman, paying no attention to the disappearing judge.

Now! Now surely Icara would say something about Miss Renshaw, about what had happened that day. But Icara said nothing. *Not now. Not ever.*

"I bet you'd like to see my bedroom," Mrs. Ellerman said to

Cubby unexpectedly. "All you little girls like to see a person's bedroom. Come on, Icky, let's show her."

Icara caught Cubby's eye and shrugged. Mrs. Ellerman steered Cubby down the hallway and then flung open a door.

"Ta-da!" she announced.

Although it had not occurred to Cubby to wonder where Mrs. Ellerman slept, as soon as she saw the room she decided at once that's what she would be when she grew up, a housekeeper for a rich person. Mrs. Ellerman not only had her own room, but also her own television and her own little refrigerator! Just like a hotel. And there was even money — not just coins, but notes, lovely new crisp notes — casually lying on the dressing table, next to a framed photo.

"That's Mrs. Ellerman's sister," said Icara. "She's a missionary on a South Sea island."

Cubby peered at the photo. Mrs. Ellerman's sister was sitting on the ground next to a coconut tree, reading what looked like a Bible to a group of children in bare feet and swimsuits.

"It's a hard life, Cubby," said Mrs. Ellerman, shaking her head. "Sooner her than me."

It didn't look like such a hard life to Cubby. At least the children in the South Seas didn't have to sit in chairs, wrapped up in blue uniforms and cashmere blazers. Cubby was sure they didn't get in trouble if they had lost their tie or the brim of their hat was broken.

"I wish I lived on an island in the South Seas," she said wistfully.

"We do live on an island in the South Seas," Icara pointed out.

But our island is too big, thought Cubby. *It doesn't feel like an island.* It felt like endless stretches of sandy, orange-yellow desert with bumps and craters and mysterious little creatures with round, shiny eyes and sharp claws flitting about in the dark.

"When I grow up," said Icara, "I'm going to live in Iceland."

"Golly," said Mrs. Ellerman, raising her eyebrows.

Iceland! Far away, far-flung, remote, isolated.

"Why would you want to live there?" asked Cubby. "It's all made of ice."

"No, it's not," said Icara. "That's what everybody thinks, but what everybody thinks isn't true. I looked it up in the encyclopedia. There's lots of grass and they have hot springs and they grow bananas inside hothouses."

"Oh," said Cubby.

"What a funny little thing you are," sighed Mrs. Ellerman affectionately.

"I'll show you," said Icara to Cubby, ignoring Mrs. Ellerman. "Come on. The encyclopedias are in my dad's study."

Reluctantly, Cubby left Mrs. Ellerman's cozy room and headed down the hallway after Icara, through another door into the judge's study. It looked like a library to Cubby, with shelves and shelves of books going up to the ceiling. There was a big square desk in the middle of the room, with a green glass top, and on the wall was an old-fashioned clock marked with Roman numerals and with a pendulum swinging under it.

Most of the books were exactly the same size and color, red with black writing on the spines.

"They're law books," said Icara, waving at them. "They're very boring—nobody can read them."

But there was another shelf with a set of encyclopedias. Icara pulled out Volume I–J and flipped it open on the desk, which was empty except for an inkwell full of black ink and a sheet of blotting paper.

"See?"

Cubby saw. Iceland in the encyclopedia was not at all icy but full of grass and flowers, and, just as Icara had said, there were photos of hothouses with banana trees and pineapple plants growing inside them.

"So why is it called Iceland?" asked Cubby, puzzled.

Icara didn't answer. She walked away from the table and closed the door of the study with a sharp click. She sat down in her father's deep, brown leather chair. It was on wheels, and she spun around on it, one complete circle, then came to a decisive stop, as though she had been waiting carefully for this moment.

"Cubby," she said, looking straight ahead at the clock on the wall above Cubby's head. "What do you think really happened?"

Cubby felt her legs lose their shape. She looked back at Icara, whose lips were still luridly pink from the ice pop.

"You mean . . ."

"To Miss Renshaw. What do you think happened to her in that cave?"

"I don't know," said Cubby helplessly.

An electric chandelier hung from the ceiling above them, rows of little glinting crystals.

"I know what I think happened," said Icara. "I'll tell you, if you tell me what you think happened."

There are no windows in this room, thought Cubby. *There must never be any sunlight.*

"I guess she got lost or something," she said, to convince herself. "She got lost. Or something."

There was a sound outside, of the front door opening and closing. Suddenly Icara became very still.

68

"She'll be back tomorrow," said Cubby, panicking. "She probably just went home or something. She got sick and went home."

Then there were footsteps going upstairs. And voices. Was it the judge?

"I don't think she'll be back tomorrow," said Icara slowly.

There were more footsteps, more voices. A door closing.

TEN

The Secret

ICARA WAS RIGHT. The next day Miss Renshaw did not come back.

Not that anybody actually said so. Nobody told them anything. The little girls only knew that Miss Renshaw had not yet returned because a new teacher appeared in the classroom. Her name was Miss Summers. She was young and had a cap of silky red hair.

"Are you instead of Miss Renshaw?" asked Elizabeth with the plaits.

"I'll be here for a little while," replied Miss Summers with a controlled smile.

She picked up the eraser and wiped Captain Cook, his voyage, and everything else right off the board with firm, vigorous strokes. When Cubby finally willed herself to look up at the board, all that remained were layers upon layers of dust. It was as though the words had never been there. *Never there,* said Cubby to herself, *never there.*

"Fractions, girls," said Miss Summers. "Let's get going."

"Yes, Miss Summers," answered the little girls, meek with gratitude at the restoration of routine, and they pulled out their fraction books and sharpened their pencils and sank into the safety of numbers.

On the playground, there were whispers everywhere, swimming about the air like tiny darting fish. Miss Renshaw had run away. No, she hadn't run away. She'd taken off her clothes and gone for a swim in the nude and been carried out to sea in a rip. No, she'd been eaten by a shark. No, it was a giant octopus. No, she'd had a nervous breakdown and been dragged off screaming to a mental hospital.

The little girls found themselves approached on all sides by older girls who would normally never even cast a downward glance at them.

"What happened? What happened to Miss Renshaw?"

"Tell us what happened. Is it true she's disappeared?"

Bethany started to cry. It was easier that way. Once she started crying, she was surrounded by comforters.

"It's all right," they said, arms reaching out and smothering her. "Don't be upset. Don't cry. Do you want to go to Matron?"

No, no, no, no! Bethany shook her head.

After the morning break, when they returned to their classroom, there was bad news. Miss Summers told them that Miss Baskerville, their headmistress, wanted to talk to them alone. Alone in the huge, echoing assembly hall. Bethany burst into tears at once. How could such a small person have so many tears? Georgina groaned and kicked the back of her chair.

"There's no need to get so upset," said Miss Summers, taken aback, because she was not used to Bethany. "Miss Baskerville just wants to have a chat, you know, about — er — about what's been happening," she finished brightly.

A chat. The little girls looked at her with pitying eyes. Poor Miss Summers. She was so new.

"Do try to stop crying, Bethany," said Miss Summers in desperation. "You'll make yourself sick."

"She's always crying," said Georgina. "We don't care," and she kicked the chair again.

Miss Summers took them down to the assembly hall at the appointed hour, eleven pairs of black shoes scuffing through sodden fig leaves. In through the double doors, lowering their heads, not looking at one another. They moved in a clump up to the front row of blue vinyl benches.

Miss Baskerville was already positioned behind the lectern on the stage, waiting for them, suspicious and magisterial. White haired, with eyes that flashed unpredictably and were sometimes, it seemed to Cubby, thick with misery. *What am I doing here?* those eyes seemed to say. *How did I get myself into this situation?*

"Sit down, girls," she said.

They sat. They knew what she was going to say. *You little girls went out into the Ena Thompson Memorial Gardens and came back to school without your teacher. I repeat, without your teacher. I would like an explanation.*

"Very well. Is everybody here?"

Cubby felt her mind waft away. Miss Baskerville's words were like music or the hum of traffic. She stared up at the huge honor boards suspended on the brick walls and read the now-familiar names, written in golden paint on the glowing wood, of girls who had won prizes years and years ago. Dulcie Adams, 1928, the Betsy Graham Memorial Prize; Muriel Mapplechat, 1941, the Miss Pamela Glissom Memorial Prize; Anne Rosenzwieg, 1954, the Enid Macanulty Memorial Prize . . .

What had happened to them all? wondered Cubby. To Dulcie, Muriel, and Anne? Or, for that matter, to Betsy and Pamela and Enid and to all those others whose heroic, shining names were unfurled there, like the names of men lost in war? What happened to all those girls once they had stepped outside the yellow gate?

They, hand in hand, with wandering steps and slow,
Through Eden took their solitary way.

Miss Renshaw had written that up on the blackboard for them to copy down in their books, to practice their italic script.

"Adam and Eve, girls," Miss Renshaw had said. "Out they went. Never, never to return."

Never, never. *Not now. Not ever.* But Cubby wouldn't think about that. She wouldn't. *You have to stop thinking — that's right.* So she stopped thinking and listened to Miss Baskerville.

"If any one of you has anything further you can say about this whole business, I need to know now," said Miss Baskerville balefully.

There was a long gray pause. Cubby looked sideways at Icara. Her possum-colored hair had fallen forward into her face, and her shirt was, as always, white and very clean. It was because she was rich. Rich people were clean. Cubby had noticed it before. When one of Icara's shirts became frayed and grubby, she bought another.

"Obviously there is more that you can say, and for some reason you are choosing not to," said Miss Baskerville, now sounding almost bored. "I fully expect at least one of you to stand up right now and tell me exactly what happened in the gardens yesterday."

Nobody stood. They couldn't, even if they wanted to. They were frozen through, frozen to the heart. *It's our little secret, girls. We won't tell anyone.*

They returned to their classroom in disgrace, without a confession. Miss Summers busied herself distributing pieces of colored paper and pots of glue to each desk.

"We're going to make collages," she told them, "in the style of Matisse."

"Who's Matisse?" asked Georgina without enthusiasm.

"Matisse was a very famous French painter," said Miss Summers, pleased to have something she could explain. "And when he was an old man, he wasn't very well, so he couldn't paint. So he lay in bed and cut pieces of colored paper and made pictures out of them."

The little girls stared at Miss Summers, at the squares of paper, out the window, at the ceiling, at the backs of one another's necks.

"Now," said Miss Summers with a frown, "who can tell me where Miss Renshaw keeps the scissors?"

Before anyone could answer, there was a knock at the door. All their eyes turned to the silver door handle, which was turning by itself as though there were a ghost pushing it. In walked the school chaplain, Reverend Broome, not in his normal blue-and-white chapel outfit but in the black leather pants and jacket that he wore to ride his motorbike. The girls stood up automatically, but they were disturbed. What was he doing here?

"If I may take a few moments of your time?" the Reverend Broome asked Miss Summers, stepping forward confidently into the room.

"Yes, of course," said Miss Summers, taken aback. "Sit down, girls, and listen to what Mr. Broome has to say."

They sat. Mr. Broome held his helmet in one hand and with the other hand he smoothed down his hair.

"Let us pray," he said, rolling forward on his toes.

They bowed their heads, amid dictionaries and rulers and the smell of paint.

"O God, by whom the meek are guided in judgment," intoned Mr. Broome, who had an unusually loud voice, especially when he was praying. "Grant us, in all our doubts and uncertainties, the grace to ask what thou would have us do."

Miss Summers did not close her eyes or even bow her head. She caught Cubby's eye. Cubby looked away.

"Amen," said Mr. Broome.

"Amen," said the eleven voices in response.

Mr. Broome stopped rocking up and down on his feet and stood up very straight, like a soldier, looking out.

"I can see every girl in this room. Every girl in this room."

This was what he always said in chapel, but here it was less impressive. After all, it was not very hard—there were only eleven of them.

"Has anyone got anything they would like to say?" said Mr. Broome.

Nobody did.

"About what happened when you went out with Miss Renshaw?"

But what did happen?

"I want you to think about it," Mr. Broome went on, drenching each word with importance. "I want you to think very hard. Very seriously. Before it's too late."

Too late. The saddest words in the English language. Cubby had read that somewhere. But were they really? There had to be sadder words—like "Your whole family has died in a horrible plague," for example.

Mr. Broome shook his head at the floor. The little girls waited. Soon he would go away. He couldn't stand there all afternoon. They could last longer than him, much longer.

"Too late," repeated Mr. Broome.

Bethany slumped forward on her desk. The Reverend Broome looked across at her, hopefully.

"Yes?"

It's our little secret.

"Nothing," said Bethany. "I just feel a bit sick."

Mr. Broome lost heart. There was something implacable about the eleven little faces in front of him — how could he hope to know their secrets?

"At any rate, I have planted a seed," he murmured to Miss Summers. "Something may come of it."

He shook her hand and smiled, then left the room quickly. They sat very still, listening to the sound of his big black motorbike boots clattering down the four flights of stairs.

The next day, a letter arrived at the homes of the eleven little girls. It was typed on a small sheet of white paper with the blue embossed school crest.

> Dear parents,
>
> You may have heard from your daughter that Miss Renshaw has been absent from school recently following a class excursion.
>
> In the immediate future it seems unlikely that Miss Renshaw will be returning to her current position. However, we have now engaged Miss Merrilee Summers to take the

girls in Miss Renshaw's absence. You will be pleased to hear that she comes with the highest qualifications.

Yours sincerely,

(Miss) Emily Baskerville
Headmistress

ELEVEN

Hiding Schoolgirl

WHEN THE MOTHERS AND FATHERS opened the envelope and read Miss Baskerville's letter, they were bewildered. What did this mean? They looked at their daughters and asked questions.

"You lost her?" said Cubby's mother. "How could you have lost her? Your teacher? I mean, I've heard of children getting lost . . ."

The mothers and fathers rang up other mothers and fathers and asked more questions. Some had even rung the school and demanded to speak to Miss Baskerville. But this was not encouraged. The situation had changed — that was all. Class 4F was no longer Class 4F. It was Class 4S, and in the morning Miss

Merrilee Summers, with her cap of silky red hair and the highest qualifications, entered the room and set them to work.

The little girls liked Miss Summers. She didn't shout. She wore nice clothes. But they missed their teacher. Miss Renshaw was gone, but she was still there with them in the room. She was there in her chair, with its worn cushion. The folders on the teacher's desk belonged to Miss Renshaw, the tin of drawing pens, the narrow vase of blue glass. She was there in the posters on the walls, in the books on the shelves, in the signs saying PENCILS, MATHEMATICS, EXTRA READING, SOCIAL STUDIES, and NATURAL SCIENCE.

They constantly expected to hear her voice. Each time Miss Summers called out to them, in the corridor or on the stairs, to stop running, stop talking, stop eating, stop shouting, stop banging, stop being so silly, it should have been Miss Renshaw calling.

Mrs. Arnold, the deputy headmistress, reappeared in their remote classroom. She knocked on the door and put her head around. At once, the little girls stood up.

"Sit down, sit down, girls," said Mrs. Arnold, waving away the courtesy.

She perched on the edge of the front desk again and looked at them over her thick-rimmed black glasses; kindly as always. They looked back. Their eyes were clear, but their hearts were dishonest.

"Now, I know you girls are feeling very upset about Miss Renshaw," Mrs. Arnold began.

Yes, yes.

"And I know you all want to do your very best to help her."

They did. They nodded, and Mrs. Arnold nodded back encouragingly.

"Now, you see, the fact of the matter is, some of you — it may be not all of you, but some of you — have something more you can tell us about what happened that day."

No nods now.

"I don't want to accuse you of hiding anything. Perhaps you don't quite understand the seriousness of the situation."

There Mrs. Arnold was quite wrong. They understood too well. *Don't say anything,* they whispered to one another, inside their heads. *Don't tell. We can't tell.*

"I know that you are all good girls," said Mrs. Arnold. "I am sure of it. And I know you want to do the right thing. You may be afraid, but you mustn't be afraid. You must do the right thing."

Oh, the right thing! It was too late for the right thing!

Mrs. Arnold stood up to go.

"You know where to find me, girls, any of you, anytime. My door is open."

She nodded at Miss Summers and was gone, coughing all the way down the four flights of stairs.

"All right then," said Miss Summers uncertainly. She had some chalk in her hand. "Let's copy down the week's spelling now, shall we?"

She turned her back on them and started to write on the blackboard. Her writing was nothing like Miss Renshaw's. It was childish and lacked Miss Renshaw's flair.

Annual
Cardigan
Eight
Fever

The little girls pulled out their spelling books and began to copy down the words. The chalk squeaked; the pages flapped.

"These words are too hard," complained Martine.

Miss Summers paid no attention. She kept on writing. They watched her back, and her hand moving across the board.

Mixed
Orphan
Socks
Unless

"I hate spelling," said Martine, and put her pencil down.

Silence.

There was a moan, and then a sob. It was Bethany. But she was not sobbing about the spelling words. Miss Summers stopped writing, put down the chalk, and turned around to face them.

"Bethany, come here," said Miss Summers. Her voice was not cross, but it was determined.

Woeful and weeping, Bethany struggled out of her chair and made her way up to the front of the room.

"Bethany," said Miss Summers, patting her arm, "I think you should go and see Mr. Dern."

Ten heads shot up in alarm, as though they were one child, with one face. No, Bethany, no!

Mr. Dern was the school counselor. He had a mustache and very short gray hair. He came to the school once a week and saw girls who had what were known as problems, in a small, cell-like square room near the chapel. Girls talked while he listened and he smoked. Girls with problems returned from these sessions stinking of nicotine and looking rather faint.

"I-I-I don't want to," spluttered Bethany through her tears. She put one of her plaits in her mouth, and her right foot turned on its side.

"Nonetheless, I think you must go," said Miss Summers, tightening her grip on the little arm. "It will be good for you to have someone to talk to."

Don't go, Bethany! they screamed silently. *Don't go!*

"I'm all right now," said Bethany in a louder voice. "I won't cry anymore." But the tears kept coming.

"I think I'd better take you there myself," said Miss Summers. "Things can't go on like this."

No, things couldn't go on like this. Bethany's shoulders slumped. Defeat was near.

"You girls sit quietly and get on with the spelling list." Miss Summers did not look at them; she kept her eyes fixed on Bethany. "I won't be long."

She half pushed, half pulled the whimpering Bethany out the door, then closed it crisply behind them.

"She's going to tell," said Georgina, jumping out of her chair as soon as they had gone. "She's going to tell—everything!"

"We're in big trouble," said the shortest Elizabeth.

Cubby trembled. Silent Deirdre put her head down on the desk. Icara got up and went over to the open window and stared out.

"Maybe it's good," said Cynthia, trying to look on the bright side, as Miss Renshaw had so often advised them. "Maybe if she tells, they'll go and find her. You know, in the cave."

They thought of the windy journey along the rocky beachfront, the waves, the naked man, the piles of rocks and shells.

"If she's still in that cave," said Icara from the window, "she must be pretty hungry by now."

Nobody spoke.

"Remember those rock paintings?" said Martine, breaking the silence.

They thought of the gloom of the wet, low-roofed cave, the firefly of Morgan's flashlight hovering about the walls.

"They were amazing," said Georgina.

Icara came away from the window and stood at the front where Miss Summers had just been.

"I don't believe they were real rock paintings, anyway," she said.

The little girls stared. What did she mean?

"I think Morgan painted them himself," said Icara.

Now they were shocked.

"Why?" asked Cynthia, mystified.

"I don't know," said Icara with a shrug. "To show off, maybe."

"Seeing is believing," said Elizabeth with the plaits firmly.

Icara was unimpressed.

"Depends on what you see," she said. "What did you see?"

What did they see? Cubby remembered with secret shame that she saw nothing, nothing at all in the flickering dark.

"It was hands," said Georgina at last. "There were hands, lots of them. Hands on the rock."

Hands, hands on the rock. A man's hand, reaching upward. Like in the Bible verse the Reverend Broome had made them learn by heart:

Behold, there ariseth a little cloud out of the sea, like a man's hand.

Bethany did not come back to class that day. She didn't dare. She went straight home after seeing Mr. Dern, without even coming back to get her bag. They knew why. Bethany was afraid. She was afraid of what they would say when they found out that she had told.

But in fact none of the little girls blamed her. Really, they were glad. The secret was over, and the truth was out.

The truth?

TWELVE

Fallen Schoolgirl

BETHANY TOLD MR. DERN, the counselor, everything. After all, Mr. Dern could make people tell him whatever he wanted, especially secrets. He listened and waited and smiled and waited and put his head on one side and waited and dragged on his cigarette and waited and it all spilled out, like egg from a cracked eggshell.

Everything.

Another letter arrived at the homes of the eleven little girls, on another small sheet of white paper with the school crest embossed in navy blue.

Dear parents,

You may have heard from your daughter that further information has come to light regarding Miss Renshaw's recent absence from school. You may rest assured that the matter is being thoroughly investigated.

Yours sincerely,

(Miss) Emily Baskerville
Headmistress

Words, words, words.

Bethany told Mr. Dern about Morgan and Miss Renshaw and the caves and the Aboriginal paintings and losing Martine's hat and getting it back again and falling over and hurting her knee and there was blood everywhere and look there's still a scab under my sock and Morgan carried me piggyback and there was a man swimming with no clothes on and it was so black in there and they were hungry and I didn't like it and Martine kept giggling and once Georgina saw Miss Renshaw and Morgan kissing.

Bethany told Mr. Dern, and Mr. Dern told Miss Baskerville, and then everybody knew.

"I need not tell you, girls: I am very disappointed."

Oh, but they were used to that.

"Very disappointed in you girls."

Weren't they always causing disappointment?

"This is not what I expect from you girls."

Letting the school down, upsetting their teachers, letting themselves down.

"Do you understand how wrong it was?"

"You have created a lot of unnecessary trouble."

"You have not been a good friend to Miss Renshaw."

"Very disappointed indeed."

Oh, but it was useless to talk to the little girls about disappointment. They knew they were disappointing; they were born to disappoint.

The police came.

"Look!" cried Cynthia in excitement, peering out the window from high up in their nest of a classroom. "It's the police!"

The police! They all ran to the window, squeezed together, and watched the big blue car come right into the playground and stop outside the steps that led to Miss Baskerville's office. The car doors opened, and out came two uniformed policemen and a man in a suit and a gray hat. Up the stairs they went, just like detectives on the television.

"Maybe they've found Miss Renshaw!"

"Maybe she's been arrested!"

"Sit down, girls, sit down. Arrested, for heaven's sake," said Miss Summers, dragging herself with difficulty away from the window. "Goodness me, what a lot of carry-on."

"They'll probably want to interview me," said Bethany importantly.

But they didn't. The police spoke to Mr. Dern, but they didn't ask for Bethany.

"He told them what I told him," Bethany explained when she found out. "So I wouldn't have to. Mr. Dern said it might tip me over the edge if I had to talk to the police."

The other little girls did not comment. Perhaps they felt that Bethany had thrown herself over the edge years ago.

"Miss Baskerville doesn't want any of us to talk to the police," said Bethany. "It would be too upsetting."

The police drove their car down to the Ena Thompson Memorial Gardens. They took a map with them, drawn by Mr. Dern with the help of Bethany, to show where the cave was.

"Are you sure you got it right?" said the tall Elizabeth. "The cave, I mean. There must be lots of caves."

Bethany looked anxious.

"I did my best!" she began to wail. "Mr. Dern said I could only do my best."

The police searched, but they found nothing. They were baffled. That's what Mrs. Arnold, the deputy headmistress, told any of the parents who called. The police were completely baffled.

"They're not the only ones," remarked Cubby's mother.

Nobody knew where Miss Renshaw had gone. Her family, who all lived in Victoria, had not seen her, not for months. None of her friends had seen her. Nobody in the Ena Thompson Memorial Gardens had seen anything the day she disappeared, or since. Nobody in the surrounding streets or the little corner shops had seen anything either. Miss Renshaw had vanished.

"Gone is gone," said Cubby's mother. "But she must have gone somewhere."

The police were not only looking for Miss Renshaw. They were also looking for Morgan. Because Morgan, too, was missing. Mr. Dern told Bethany and Bethany told them.

"Morgan hasn't gone back to work," said Bethany. "Nobody knows where he is."

"What about his family?" asked Georgina.

Did Morgan have a family? A wife, children? A mother and a father? It was hard to imagine.

"He never said anything about his family," said Martine, struggling to remember. "Did he?"

"He said he grew up in the desert," said Icara, balancing on one leg of her chair. "With a tribe of Aborigines. Ha, ha."

"The army might be looking for him, as well as the police," said Elizabeth with the plaits. "Remember how Miss Renshaw said he refused to join the army? But they come and get you, don't they?"

But these things were too deep and difficult for the little girls. After all, they knew nothing of wives or armies or desert tribes. At night on the television news they heard gunfire and the sound of helicopter blades and bombs falling. Soldiers were dying in flames far away in a black-and-white land where people wore triangular hats and worked in rice fields and everyone, everyone, was always running away in terror. That was all they knew, all they could know. The little girls hung on to the brink of a hugeness that they knew was there but had no way of discovering.

They were sad, so very sad. Miss Summers tried hard. She thought of lots of interesting things to teach them. They learned about the Bushmen of the Kalahari Desert and the invention of Hindu-Arabic numerals and the life cycle of the garden snail. They made Indonesian shadow puppets, and towers out of empty cans, and coconut ice in pink and green. But still they were so sad. Miss Summers paced the classroom floor and kept trying, but her smile grew thinner.

"I wouldn't be surprised if that Miss Summers of yours goes off with her highest qualifications to find a job in another school," said Cubby's mother.

In the corner of the classroom, up high near the ceiling, was a small gray box. This was a loudspeaker that had a connection to a microphone in an office downstairs. Usually the voice that came out of the box was friendly and familiar — an announcement about sports, or lunch specials, or a reminder to bring money for an excursion, or donations for the Harvest Festival.

But every now and then, only when something really bad had happened, the voice of Miss Baskerville herself would come crackling out of the gray box and fill the room and everyone in it with fear.

That's what they were waiting for. Their eyes wandered up to the gray box a hundred times a day. *Any moment now,* they thought, looking up with respect and dread, the voice would come. Miss Baskerville would speak, and then they would know what had really happened.

Any moment now.

THIRTEEN

Schoolgirl and Man

IT WAS NOT A VOICE IN THE END, but a face. The face was on
the front page of the afternoon newspaper, piles and piles and
piles of them, in the kiosk at the bus stop. Cubby saw it there
as she stood waiting to buy sherbet-filled lollies after school. A
small, smudgy face. When she saw it, she felt as though an icicle
was slipping under her ribs. The headline read:

TEACHER MISSING

And the face underneath it was Morgan's.

Cubby read the black words on the page. Morgan was a bad
person. The newspaper knew everything about him, how bad

he was. Morgan had been in prison. Morgan had done terrible things. Morgan was not his real name, the newspaper said. He had another name when he did the bad things. He had done those things and he had been sent to prison. He had been in prison for a long time.

"What was she doing with that fellow?" said Cubby's mother. "And all of you little girls? It's unbelievable."

It was unbelievable. They couldn't believe it.

"You could all have been killed!" said Cubby's mother.

But we weren't, thought Cubby. *We're all here, and Miss Renshaw isn't.*

A third small white note came home.

Dear parents,

With regard to the absence of Miss Renshaw from school, you may have seen references to this matter in the press recently. I am sure that you agree that it is best that both girls and parents refrain from speaking to any members of the press, in the unlikely event that anyone should be approached.

Yours sincerely,

(Miss) Emily Baskerville
Headmistress

"What's the press?" asked Martine.

"The press means newspaper and television and radio journalists," explained Miss Summers, pushing her fingers against her forehead.

"What's a journalist?" asked the shortest Elizabeth.

"It's someone who writes the news," said Miss Summers. "A journalist goes out and discovers what's happened, then writes it down for the newspaper to print."

"Like Clark Kent," said Martine.

"Not like Clark Kent," said Miss Summers sharply. "Clark Kent is not a real person. A journalist is a real person. You girls are not to speak to anyone like that. Nobody with cameras, microphones, or notebooks. You are not to speak to anyone like that."

"That's a bit rude, though, isn't it?" Georgina objected. "I mean, if an adult asks us something, isn't it polite to answer?"

"You are not to speak to anyone like that," repeated Miss Summers. "Miss Baskerville has forbidden it."

When they were alone, the little girls huddled together in horror.

"Miss Renshaw said he was a poet," said Elizabeth with the plaits. "She never said he had been in prison."

"Do you think she knew?"

Of course she knew; that's why she liked him. Miss Renshaw loved prisoners. After all, it was in the Bible:

I was sick, and ye visited me: I was in prison, and ye came unto me.

"But he wasn't in prison anymore," Georgina objected. "It says in the paper he was let out of prison. You're only supposed to visit prisoners when they're locked up."

"How can you be out of prison if you've done something like that?" said Cynthia. "He kidnapped someone."

And worse.

"I don't think she knew," said Bethany, who had stopped crying, for a while at least. "She'd be too scared. What if he did it again?"

We won't mention these little meetings with Morgan to our parents or other staff, will we, girls? We won't mention Morgan. Will we?

"He's a bad person," said Martine.

Then the news came that the police had found something in the cave. Something important. The little girls knew because the police told Mr. Dern and Mr. Dern told Bethany.

"Mr. Dern said he'd tell me as soon as he knows anything more," said Bethany as they crowded around her.

What could the police have found?

"Footprints," said Georgina.

"Maybe bones," said Martine.

They shuddered.

"Whose bones?" said Icara. "It takes ages to turn into bones. Months and months."

But it wasn't bones. Mr. Dern told Bethany and Bethany told them. It was the necklace, the tear-shaped amber bead that hung around Miss Renshaw's neck. The police found it lying on the floor of the cave. The leather string was broken, snapped in two. The police picked everything up in gloved hands. They sealed the pieces in a plastic bag and put it on a shelf marked EVIDENCE.

"Mr. Dern said they're checking it for fingerprints," said Bethany.

Fingerprints . . .

"She probably just dropped it on the ground and forgot about it," said Georgina. "It doesn't mean anything."

Icara had been sitting by herself at the back of the classroom. Icara, remote, isolated, distant, far-flung. But now she got up, and with her hands in her blazer pockets, she sauntered down the aisle to where Bethany was slumped forward on her desk, surrounded by the other girls. Bethany looked up apprehensively.

"You've got to face facts," said Icara.

Icara is a realist, but the world needs dreamers.

"What do you mean?" said Bethany.

"The truth is," said Icara, "the police think Miss Renshaw is dead."

The room held its breath, scandalized. Then out tumbled a medley of outrage.

"Don't be mean! That's horrible."

"Miss Renshaw is not dead! Don't say that! How can you say that?"

"You don't know! Don't listen to her. It's not true!"

The voices came from everywhere. Icara stood with her feet apart, steady on the ground.

"It's been too long," she said. "If she was alive, we'd know by now."

"Not if she was hiding on purpose," said Martine.

Icara looked at her scornfully. "Why would she do that?"

"People do hide in caves," retorted Martine, "for your information," as though this sort of thing happened all the time on the Isle of Pines.

"Why didn't they find her, then?" said Icara. "Why did they only find the necklace?"

For a moment they all saw it, the delicate, nearly invisible remains of the winged insect trapped in amber, millions of years ago.

"What do you think happened, then?" asked Cubby.

Icara turned and looked straight at her.

"I think Morgan murdered her," she said. "Down in that cave. That's why they want the fingerprints."

Sickness spread from one child to another.

"But he loved her," said Georgina. "I saw them kissing."

The kiss. A kiss means love. Morgan loved Miss Renshaw. Down in the cave with the Aboriginal paintings, under the grand Moreton Bay fig, at the water's edge, in front of the wild Pacific Ocean, he kissed Miss Renshaw and he loved her.

"But he was a poet," said the tall Elizabeth. "He wrote poems."

"And he was a gardener," put in another Elizabeth. "He loved living things . . . ." She trailed off.

"He probably learned all that in prison," replied Icara, shrugging. "That's what you do in prison. You learn things so that you can get a job when they let you out."

"But he was against killing," said Cynthia. "That's why he wouldn't go to the war, remember?"

She stopped, troubled. From what they had read in the newspapers, it seemed unlikely that Morgan would have been made to go in the army at all. He'd been in prison until just a little while ago. They wouldn't put someone like that in the army, would they?

Cubby tried to remember Morgan's face, but all she could bring to mind were his gentle fingers covered with earth and the sound of his voice, singing like rocking waves.

"But why?" she said. "Why would he do that?"

"People just do," said Icara. "Some people just murder people," said Icara, the realist. "They don't need a reason; they just do it."

Dead, dead. Could Miss Renshaw be dead? Swallowed up, disappeared, dead?

"You're wrong—you're so wrong," said Bethany, clenching her little white hands into fists. "Miss Renshaw is not dead. She's coming back. I know she is."

Cubby stared up at the blackboard. Words are never really wiped away, she realized. They're always there, under all the layers of chalk dust. Thousands and thousands of words had been written on this board, hundreds of thousands.

Not now. Not ever.

"I know she's coming back," said Bethany.

All the words Miss Renshaw had ever written might have been wiped meticulously away by Miss Summers, but they were still there, Cubby knew it, in chalky, invisible layer upon layer underneath. Every word.

They weren't just written; she could hear them. She could hear the words, right in her ear. Someone was there, in the room with her, speaking right in her ear, and her nose and mouth were filled with the strong, sweet smell of Morgan's cigarettes.

FOURTEEN

Ebb and Flow

THE LITTLE GIRLS TURNED AWAY from Icara. They couldn't
help it. It was too much. But Cubby found she couldn't turn
away, not entirely.

When the bell rang for the end of school, the others left
with their arms around one another, whispering. Then the room
was empty, except for the two of them, each at her own desk,
putting her things away. Cubby closed her bag slowly, clicking
the buckles shut one at a time. She could feel Icara looking at
her, and those unseen eyes seemed to be asking something,
almost begging. *Help me,* the eyes said. *Please.* But that made no
sense. Icara didn't need any help. She never cried. She was the
strongest of them all.

Cubby looked up. Icara was standing next to her desk.

"Can you come over to my house again, this afternoon?" said Icara. "There's something I want to show you."

"All right," said Cubby.

And so she found herself for the second time leaving the school with Icara, heading past the uniform inspection at the yellow gate, down the hill and onto the bus, then on again through the winding streets to the last leafy stop. Icara pulled the cord, and they dragged their schoolbags down the bus steps.

The afternoon air was warm, and full of invisible birds. They ambled through the tunnel of trees along the road. This time there was a sleek green car parked outside Icara's house and the gate was swinging open. Icara took out her key, and in they went through the front door, letting their bags drop on the floor.

"Don't take off your shoes this time," said Icara quickly. "I want to show you something outside."

There was no sign of Mrs. Ellerman, just a bottle of orange juice open on the kitchen counter. The two girls headed out the glass door into the backyard.

"It's down at the river," said Icara.

At the river? They could see the river from where they stood, but between the yard and the water, there was a stretch of wild bushes.

"There's a hidden path," said Icara, answering Cubby's unspoken question.

They walked to the edge of the bushes, and Icara held up a knotted branch. Behind it was the beginning of a pathway, covered in mud and leaves. They made their way down cautiously, as it was steep, so steep in some places that they had to half slide. Stinging branches flicked back in their faces. It wasn't far — Cubby could smell the closeness of the mangroves. Another branch smacked her in the ear, and suddenly the path ended and the river stretched out before them, as shining and black as the night sky.

"Over there," said Icara. "That's what I wanted to show you."

She was pointing to a metal pole, just along the riverbank. Tied to the pole, to stop it from floating away, was a little blue wooden rowboat.

"It belongs to the people next door," said Icara. She gestured with her elbow at the tiled roof of a neighboring house just discernible through the dense forest of eucalypts. "But we can borrow it."

A boat!

"We could row down the river for a bit," said Icara. "I've done it before. We could explore."

On the other side of the river, as far as Cubby could see, there were no houses, only bush and mud. It looked like a place where people had never been.

The tide surged backward and forward, mild but relentless.

"Let's go," said Cubby, excited.

They took off their shoes, tucked their socks inside them, and laid them on a high rock away from the water. Then they stepped out into the shallows toward the boat. It bobbed away from them each time they got close, like a shy pony. Eventually

Icara managed to hold it steady and they scrambled in. It smelled of grass and fish.

"I'll do the rowing," said Icara, moving herself onto the bench in the middle. "You sit at the back."

She lifted off the rope to release the boat from the metal pole. Then she picked up the two wooden oars, fit them into the oarlocks, dipped them into the river with a slicing splash, and began to row.

Cubby sat on the back bench on a wet plastic cushion. She let her fingers hang over the side, touching the surface of the icy water with her fingertips. The oars swished and gulped. The little boat twisted through the reeds until it eased out into freedom as Icara rowed on.

The river began to narrow. The banks on both sides were overgrown with bush and trees, peeling paperbarks, and low, creeping mangroves.

We could be anywhere, thought Cubby dreamily. *We could have gone back in time, thousands of years.*

They were being borne along with the help of a tidal pull— Cubby could feel it dragging through her fingers. Translucent jellyfish swam alongside the boat, so close she could touch them.

"Look," said Icara.

Cubby opened her eyes. Had she been asleep? She must have, because it seemed as though the sun was setting, black and orange, and the green of the bush had become stone gray and the water around them blended in with the coming night. But it was too early for sunset—how had it become so dark so quickly?

"What time is it?" she said, sitting up.

"Look," said Icara insistently. "Over there."

Cubby looked. Icara stopped rowing, letting the oars sit in the oarlocks. The boat swayed up and down. Cubby saw a tire suspended from a tree branch that hung over the water, for swinging and jumping. Behind the tire on the riverbank, half hidden by a tangle of twigs and fallen branches, was a wooden cutout figure of a deer with pale painted spots. Next to it was a sign, falling down on one side. It said, WELCOME TO FAIRYLAND.

"What is it?" asked Cubby.

"Fairyland," whispered Icara.

The boat floated farther on. Peering out from the depths of the gum trees stood a flat and faded wooden Snow White, black hair, blue dress, pink skin, red lips.

"It looks so old," said Cubby.

"It is old," said Icara. "It's like a picnic place. It closed down. Ages ago."

The boat drifted.

"I had a birthday party there," said Icara, "when I was six. There are swings and things. And a flying fox."

The boat was being drawn through the water toward the riverbank, closer and closer to the wooden figures and the collapsing sign.

"My mother was there," said Icara. "At the party."

So Icara's mother had not always been in Los Angeles. She

had been married to the judge, and they had lived together with Icara, just like everybody else's family.

"Was it good?" asked Cubby shyly. "The party?"

Swish, swish, swish.

"Everybody was happy," replied Icara.

Cubby felt a shift of fear; she didn't know why. The Snow White figure was too near, the peeling smile too sweet. She could see the wood rotting in the growing darkness. Something rustled deep in the ferns.

"It's late — it must be so late," she said. "Let's go back."

Icara didn't answer. Her eyes were fixed on the swaying water. The trees on either side of the river had become shadows — they had lost all their color. She turned to Cubby, two dimly shining eyes.

"Do you believe in ghosts, Cubby?" she asked.

Thicker than shadows, the trees were like walls closing in on either side.

I don't know, said Cubby inside her head. I don't know.

Not now. Not ever.

Worse than walls, they were black and huge, like claws moving forward with predatory, scratching sounds.

"Let's go home," said Cubby, terrified. "Please, Icara. Let's go home."

Icara sighed, such a deep sigh. She lifted the oars and began to row. She rowed away from the sharp claws and away from the trembling Snow White, back toward the house. Little lights shone at a distance, each moment getting closer. Cubby's heartbeat began to slow; the danger was passing.

They didn't speak at all, not on the journey back, not as they pulled the boat to the shore of the little beach, not as they found their dry shoes and socks on the rock and put them on, not as they made their way up the path through the bushes to the house. It was as though they had been drained of language.

As they came nearer to the house, they heard the sound of the television singing out advertisements into the night air. It was so late! Cubby would have to ring her mother at once to let her know where she was before getting the bus home.

But when they came in, it wasn't Mrs. Ellerman sitting with her sewing on her lap, watching television. It wasn't the judge, with his newspaper and his cigarette. It was Amanda-fit-to-be-loved, lying on the sofa staring at the flashing screen, in jeans and a T-shirt. And with her golden hair all the way down to her waist, thick and loose, like fur.

"Hello," said Amanda, looking up briefly at them.

Icara did not stop walking. She kept walking, right through the room, up the stairs, door closed, gone. Cubby stood there helplessly.

"Hello," said Cubby.

Amanda tugged languidly on a silver bracelet around her wrist. At school you weren't allowed to wear any jewelry, but they were not at school now.

"You're a friend of Icara's, aren't you?" she asked.

"Yes," said Cubby.

"I'm a family friend," said Amanda, and she reached out to change the television channel.

Cubby went to the hat stand by the front door and picked

up her bag. There was no sign of Icara coming down to say good-bye, no sign of anyone. So she opened the door and left by herself. She walked to the bus stop through the lamp-lit street, past the vines that gripped the high sandstone walls.

She did not have to wait long. The bus approached with its white blinding eyes. Cubby mounted the steps and the door hissed shut, and she was carried away, into the night.

FIFTEEN

Window Shadow

THE NEXT DAY, AFTER THE MORNING BELL RANG, the little girls were scattered about the classroom, waiting for Miss Summers. Icara sat at her desk, clean, possum haired, straight backed. She had a book out and was reading. She didn't say hello to Cubby or even look at her.

They heard footsteps.

"Miss Summers is coming!" called out the shortest Elizabeth.

The girls ran to stand behind their desks, to be ready as the door opened. Still reading, Icara got to her feet. Miss Summers came in with a wad of white paper in her arms. But she was not alone. Into the classroom with her came Miss Baskerville.

The little girls could feel each other quaking. This had never happened before! Miss Baskerville had never been in their classroom. It was such a long way up, after all, four flights of stairs. Why had she come now? It was bad. It could only be bad.

"Good morning, girls," said Miss Baskerville.

"Good morning, Miss Baskerville," they replied in unison, in small, shaking voices.

"Sit down, girls," said Miss Baskerville.

They sat. It must be about Miss Renshaw. Perhaps the police had found her! Miss Renshaw and Morgan must have got lost somehow in that low, dripping cave, but they must have made their way out. Probably Miss Renshaw was too upset to come herself—after all, she would want to have a bath and something to eat first. What else would bring their headmistress up four flights of stairs? Miss Renshaw was back!

But they didn't believe it, not a word. They waited.

Miss Baskerville walked into the middle of the room, coming to a stop in front of the blackboard, slightly bending forward, as though she were making up her mind what to say. She looked so very old. Well, she was old. It was an old world, and every day it grew older.

"Girls," said Miss Baskerville, "I've come up here because I want to speak to you all, alone, separately from the rest of the school."

Miss Summers laid her wad of white papers down on the desk and stood next to the half-open window. Outside, the sky was soft with clouds and sunlight.

"I want to speak to you about Miss Renshaw," said Miss Baskerville. "The police have been to see me."

The clouds seemed to move slightly closer, as if they wanted to hear what was being said.

"This is what the police have told me," said Miss Baskerville. "Miss Renshaw has been missing for nearly ten days now. This is a long time for someone to be missing. When someone has been missing a long time like this, there are a number of things you can think."

Miss Baskerville stopped, and started again.

"One is that the person has gone away for some private, personal reason and for that same reason does not tell anyone where they have gone. This is possibly what has happened with Miss Renshaw."

Bethany turned and glared triumphantly at Icara. But Icara was reading her book, hidden under her desk.

"The police think it is unlikely that Miss Renshaw would go away without telling anyone, and I must say I agree with them."

Wind from the harbor came through the open window. Miss Summers put her hand over the ream of white paper on her desk to stop the sheets from blowing away.

"Another reason a person goes missing and no word is heard from them is that they are no longer alive."

Miss Summers closed the window with a screech and a thud.

"It is possible," said Miss Baskerville, "that Miss Renshaw is no longer alive."

Dead.

"Now, I know that is a very upsetting thought. It is very upsetting for you. For all of us."

Ah, the tears were streaming.

"When people are upset, there are some things we can do to help us cope. So that is why I have decided we will have a service on Thursday in the chapel."

A funeral?

"It is not a funeral," said Miss Baskerville. "It will be a special kind of service in which we will remember Miss Renshaw and her life in the school. I wanted to tell you little girls first, so that you will be ready for this. Your parents are able to attend as well. There has been a note sent home, giving all these details."

Miss Baskerville looked at them, searchingly, as though there was something they could tell her, some knowledge they were willfully withholding. But mostly she looked sad.

"Now, does anyone have any questions?"

Obediently, to fill in the space, Georgina put up her hand.

"Do we have to wear our blazers?"

"Yes," said Miss Baskerville.

Cynthia put up her hand.

"What time does it start?"

"The service will begin straight after roll call," said Miss Baskerville.

Martine put up her hand.

"Can we go home with our parents afterward? When it's over?"

"Yes," said Miss Baskerville. "If your parents speak with Miss Summers before leaving the school grounds."

Bethany put up her hand. Her cheeks were very pink, swamped with blood.

"Yes, Bethany?" said Miss Baskerville.

"I still think Miss Renshaw will come back one day," said Bethany simply.

How quiet the room was. A seagull came to rest on the windowsill just outside. Its beak was bright red, and so were its eyes. It pecked with its beak against the glass.

"I know this is a very sad time," said Miss Baskerville after a pause. "Very sad. But the important thing in life is to move forward. That is the best and kindest thing you can do for Miss Renshaw now, to show her what fine, brave young women you are."

The final note came home to their parents, on crisp, white paper, embossed with the school crest.

Dear parents,

I am writing to let you know that there will be a memorial service in the chapel for Miss Renshaw this coming Thursday morning. The service will commence promptly at 9 a.m. and last for approximately 40 minutes. Parents may attend with their daughters, if they wish.

Yours sincerely,

(Miss) Emily Baskerville
Headmistress

SIXTEEN

Holding Hands

IT FELT WRONG TO BE GOING into chapel with parents. Parents shouldn't be anywhere in the school, really, let alone the chapel. It felt like Speech Day. Not that too many parents ended up coming. When Cubby's mother read the letter, she blinked and said, "Would you like me to come, Cubby?" but Cubby shook her head. No, no, she didn't want anyone to be there. She didn't want to be there herself.

But some parents did come. The youngest Elizabeth's parents came — they were the sort of parents that came to everything. Martine's mother came, dressed in a pantsuit and with silver-purple hair. Silent Deirdre's very tall father came.

And the judge came, with Mrs. Ellerman.

"Hello, Cubby," said the judge. He nodded solemnly. Mrs. Ellerman winked and squeezed Cubby's shoulder.

"Cheer up, darling—don't be miserable," she said. "You can sit with me."

I must look miserable, thought Cubby, surprised, because she didn't feel it. She wanted to, she tried to, but somehow all the dense sadness around her filled up the space, and she found that she had no feelings left.

"Thought I'd come along, you know," said Mrs. Ellerman. "Show a bit of support. Dear me."

The organ played softly as they filed up the stairs, notes spilling into the open hallways, out from the doors of the chapel. Amanda-fit-to-be-loved, glorious and golden and so very far from death, stood at the entrance as part of her duties as a prefect, passing out hymnbooks. Her hair was tied back and her jewelry hidden or removed. The judge took a book from her and went and sat down, Icara beside him.

Cubby found herself shepherded along by Mrs. Ellerman to the same pew. She hoped Icara didn't mind her sitting with them. Icara had hardly spoken a word to her, or anyone, really, since that afternoon on the boat. She was always reading, or looking in the other direction. As though she were angry. Cubby tried to catch her eye, but Icara turned her head away.

"You tell me what to do, darling," whispered Mrs. Ellerman, digging Cubby in the ribs as they sat down. "I wouldn't have a clue."

Cubby did not have a clue herself. She had never been to a memorial service before. She had never known anyone who had died, except for Agamemnon, and you don't have memorial services for guinea pigs.

"These are nice," said Mrs. Ellerman, pointing to the row of little cushions hung on hooks on the back of the pew in front of them.

They were kneelers, embroidered by Old Girls of the school. Some were very modest, with simply a cross or an emblem of one of the schoolhouses. But others were more lavish and Mrs. Ellerman–like, showing mysterious biblical animals in strangely bright colors.

"Very nice work," said Mrs. Ellerman, impressed. "What are they for?"

"They're to kneel on," said Cubby, as embarrassed as if Mrs. Ellerman were her own mother. "You know, when you pray, so you don't hurt your knees."

But Mrs. Ellerman drew the line at kneeling.

"With my sciatica? Are you crazy?"

Amanda-fit-to-be-loved, having finished handing out the hymnbooks, took her place in the pew just in front of them. The music of the organ suddenly changed tempo and became very loud. The Reverend Broome swept into the chapel in his robes, followed by Miss Baskerville and Mrs. Arnold. Everyone stood.

"Hymn number 228 in the hymnbook," said Mr. Broome in his usual rousing voice. "Let us join together and sing."

"Jerusalem the golden
With milk and honey blest,

Beneath thy contemplation
Sink heart and voice opprest."

Cubby sang along as best she could, but it was funny hearing the judge's deep voice singing next to her. In any case, Mrs. Ellerman soon lost concentration and dug her in the ribs again.

"I like those windows!"

Obediently, Cubby looked up at the subdued stained-glass image of Jesus surrounded by children, their translucent gray-glass faces and hair the color of honey, like the amber bead that hung around Miss Renshaw's neck.

"I know not, oh, I know not
What joys await me there!
What radiancy of glory
What bliss beyond compare!"

"Please be seated," said the Reverend Broome when the hymn had finished, and they sat, Miss Baskerville and Mrs. Arnold on special seats at the front where everyone could see them and their serious, sad faces.

Mr. Broome stepped over to the lectern. It was in the shape of a wooden eagle with glittering eyes and a curved beak. The big black-and-gold Bible was spread across its wings. Mr. Broome read aloud, almost shouting:

"Lo! I tell you a mystery. We shall not all sleep, but we shall
all be changed, in a moment, in the twinkling of an eye, at the

last trumpet. For the trumpet will sound, and the dead will be
raised imperishable."

He looked up from the Bible and calmly surveyed the room. Then he left the eagle and strode onto the red carpet at the front, swirling across the floor in his white robes like an ancient Roman senator.

"Girls, parents, teachers. I want to speak to you today about Miss Renshaw."

"About time!" whispered Mrs. Ellerman.

"Miss Renshaw was born in Wangaratta."

"Ah, a Victorian lass," Mrs. Ellerman said, nodding.

Is Mrs. Ellerman going to keep speaking through the entire sermon? wondered Cubby in desperation.

"Miss Renshaw loved her work," continued the Reverend Broome. "She was a passionate and committed teacher."

"She was passionate, all right," said Mrs. Ellerman dryly.

"Hers is a tragedy that has touched our whole school community. A life so rich and promising . . ."

"Promises, promises," said Mrs. Ellerman to Cubby.

"Sucked down into the bowels of the earth."

The judge coughed slightly.

"Bit fruity," agreed Mrs. Ellerman.

"She was greatly loved by the girls . . ."

Bethany began to sob. Mrs. Arnold and Miss Baskerville exchanged glances.

". . . and greatly appreciated by the staff for her original mind."

Mrs. Arnold made a sign. Somebody took Bethany out; she was sobbing just too loudly.

"Thank heavens," said Mrs. Ellerman.

Miss Baskerville coughed and moved in her seat. The Reverend Broome subsided. Spent, he returned to his seat and knelt down on his own special kneeler.

"Let us pray," said the Reverend Broome.

Cubby and Icara knelt and bent their heads, but the judge and Mrs. Ellerman stayed firmly seated. Prayer followed prayer followed prayer. The Reverend Broome prayed for the girls and for the school and for the government and for the queen and for anyone else he could think of, it seemed to Cubby, and they knelt together with their eyes closed and listened to Mr. Broome's purring tones until finally it was over.

The organ started again, almost imperceptibly, like breathing. Everyone stood up. Miss Baskerville and Mrs. Arnold went first, out the side entrance, pursued rapidly by Mr. Broome.

"Well, as my old dad used to say," remarked Mrs. Ellerman as they made their way down the aisle to the front entrance, "if you've read the Bible, nothing in life can possibly surprise you."

There was a delay leaving the chapel, as the door was narrow and everyone tried to leave at once. As Cubby squeezed herself into the hallway, Icara sidled up to her.

"Do you want to come with us?" she said. "My dad's taking us out to lunch."

"Oh." Cubby looked down at her shoes, not sure what to say. After all, Icara had not spoken to her, or even looked at her, since they had been out in the boat together.

"In a restaurant," said Icara. "Do you want to come?"

"Am I allowed?" asked Cubby.

"Mrs. Ellerman will tell Miss Summers," said Icara. "We'll drop you back at school afterwards."

It was decided, then.

"All right," said Cubby.

Icara reached out and took Cubby's surprised hand. She held it in her own, all the way down the stairs, onto the playground, and out beyond the yellow gate. She held it so tightly, as though she were afraid that if she let go, Cubby might turn around and run away.

SEVENTEEN

Mythological Fish

THE JUDGE WAS ALREADY outside the school, waiting for them in his green car, with Mrs. Ellerman sitting on the front seat next to him. He had one hand on the steering wheel, and with the other he was shielding his eyes from the sun. He was looking upward, at a fire escape that clung to the outer wall of the school. Right at the top of the stairs stood Amanda-fit-to-be-loved, watching them, like a sentinel on a tower, as the car pulled away.

They drove into the city and parked at the back of a restaurant that was down a lane of shops. Cubby had never been to such a place before. The walls were hung with paintings of people with no clothes on, and there was a fish tank, lit up and bubbling, with crabs inside it, and another tank with long-finned goldfish swirling like dancers in and out of a craggy plastic castle. Waiters stood about in bow ties, white shirts, and black jackets.

"What would you like to drink, Cubby?" asked the judge as they sat at a round table laid with sparkling cutlery and glasses and napkins folded in the shape of peaked hats.

"Coca-Cola," said Mrs. Ellerman confidently. "That's what the young ones like."

A waiter came up behind her and helped Cubby push her chair under the table. Then he whisked up her napkin and stretched it out across her lap. The judge nodded at the waiter, who almost instantly brought two enormous glasses for Icara and Cubby, and a bottle of white wine, which he poured out for the judge and Mrs. Ellerman.

"Dear, oh, dear, poor lady," said Mrs. Ellerman, raising her glass, in tribute to Miss Renshaw.

Cubby and Icara drank. There were so many bubbles that Cubby was afraid she was going to sneeze, so she held her breath. The judge took off his jacket. Underneath he wore a pink striped shirt and cuff links made of round black stones. He tapped the menu, which was cased in leather like an expensive book.

"Now, then, what would you like to eat?"

"Can I have an omelette and chips?" said Icara.

"You may," replied the judge. "Cubby?"

"Oh, just the same," said Cubby, looking down at her reflection in the surface of a large spoon.

"Let's all have an omelette, then," said the judge. "What do you say, Mrs. Ellerman?"

"Lovely," said Mrs. Ellerman, beaming.

The waiter brought them bread and butter and bowls of salad. Nobody spoke much. The judge occasionally murmured something to Mrs. Ellerman, who gestured in reply. Icara didn't say a word, and Cubby didn't know how to. The whole time, people arrived at the restaurant laughing and chatting, and plates and glasses clinked and clattered. It sounded like music, like violins tuning up before a concert.

The omelette and chips were delicious. When they finished eating, the waiter took away their empty plates. The judge wiped his mouth neatly with his napkin.

"Well, well," he said.

"Well, indeed," said Mrs. Ellerman. "Did you enjoy that, Cubby?"

"Yes, thank you," replied Cubby politely, although she wished there had been more chips.

"Now, I'm sure you girls would like some ice cream." Mrs. Ellerman widened her eyes at them. "Or a cake. Come on, Icky, you come with me. Let's go over to the trolley and pick something lovely for Cubby."

Icara stood up and followed Mrs. Ellerman to the dessert trolley in the middle of the room. It was laden with wonderful-looking cakes, layers of chocolate and cream in bowls, colored jellies, and glass dishes of meringues and fruit. Cubby wished she could have gone with them. She didn't want to be sitting alone with the judge. She had the feeling the judge was going to say something to her, something she didn't want to hear.

The judge reached into the top pocket of his beautiful shirt and took out a cigarette packet with a camel on it. He carefully removed a slim cigarette and lit it with a match from a book of matches on the table.

"I'm so glad, Cubby," said the judge, breathing out a mouthful of smoke, "that you are Icara's friend."

The cigarette crackled, and the end of it grew bright and hot.

"I worry about Icara, naturally," said the judge.

Cubby nervously licked her lips, which tasted of salt. She supposed it was natural. Fathers worried about lots of things.

"It's been very hard for her, I know," said the judge.

"Um, you mean, because of Miss Renshaw?" said Cubby, as he seemed to expect her to say something.

"Ah, Miss Renshaw, yes, well, poor Miss Renshaw." The judge shook his head. "That was a terrible business, of course. But it's not Miss Renshaw I'm referring to."

If only Icara and Mrs. Ellerman would return with the desserts. Why were they taking so long?

"You mean, um, her mother?" said Cubby. Was that what he wanted her to say?

"Her mother," said the judge, nodding at once. So that was it. "Yes, her mother. Now, tell me, Cubby, does she talk much about her mother?"

"Well, um," said Cubby. "Not really. Um."

The judge ashed his cigarette in the round metal ashtray.

"Just, you know, that she lives in Los Angeles and everything," said Cubby.

She didn't want to say the word *divorce*. That wasn't the sort of thing you could say out loud, especially not to an adult.

"In Los Angeles," repeated the judge.

There was a quiet bubbling of water from the fish tank. The judge stubbed out his cigarette. He picked up an apple from a plate of fruit that had been placed by a waiter in the center of the table. With a curved little silver knife, he began to cut the apple into thin half-moons. He looked very sad, quite suddenly, as if sadness had fallen like a curtain across his face.

"But she doesn't live in Los Angeles," said the judge.

Away swam a fish, into the sunken castle.

"She's dead."

Swish, swish.

"She died when Icara was six."

Swish.

"Perhaps you misunderstood," said the judge.

Cubby realized now that, of course, she had misunderstood. Icara might have told her that her mother lived in Los Angeles, but really, how could anyone live in Los Angeles? This was a mythical city, a city that existed only in films and newspapers. People like them couldn't live there. Any more than they could live in Fairyland. . . .

"We got Bombe Alaska," said Icara, appearing back at the table. She slid a bowl in front of Cubby. "It's like meringue with ice cream inside."

"No cheesecake, I'm afraid," said Mrs. Ellerman to the

judge, "so I got you some nice strawberry mousse instead."

Cubby looked across at the green, bright water of the fish tank. She picked up a spoon and began to eat the meringue, but afterward she could not remember what it tasted like. It was like eating air.

When the meal was over, they left the restaurant and got into the judge's car to take Cubby back to school. Nobody spoke on the drive, not even Mrs. Ellerman. Icara pushed herself into the corner of the backseat and stared out through the open window at the traffic. The judge came to a stop outside the yellow gate, but he did not turn the engine off.

"Will you be all right to get home now, Cubby?" he asked, looking at her in the rearview mirror.

"Yes, I'm fine," said Cubby. She opened the back door and got out. "Thank you for lunch."

Mrs. Ellerman gave Cubby a jaunty wave.

"Good-bye, Cubby."

"Bye, Icara," said Cubby.

"Bye," replied Icara from the corner of the backseat.

The car swept away down the street. As she watched it go, it seemed to Cubby that Icara was even now out in the little boat on the river, sailing past the darkness of Fairyland, where pale jellyfish floated just beneath the surface and the river lapped over the edges of the world.

And in the shadow of the tall house the judge stood at the doorway, sadly cutting his apple into thin moons, with the golden hair of Amanda-fit-to-be-loved spread out radiantly behind him.

1975

NEW SOUTH WALES DEPARTMENT OF EDUCATION
HIGHER SCHOOL CERTIFICATE EXAMINATION 1975
Ancient History
Paper 1 Thucydides Option

NOTE: Use a separate writing booklet clearly marked
Paper 1 Question 1 (Greek)

At last, when many dead now lay piled one upon another in the stream, and part of the army had been destroyed at the river, and the few that escaped from thence cut off by the cavalry, Nicias surrendered himself to Gylippus.
THUC. VII.85

To what extent can Nicias personally be held responsible
for the Athenian defeat at Sicily?

EIGHTEEN

Always Teatime

THE TIME WAS UP. The hands on the clock had reached four o'clock. It was over.

"Pens down, girls."

Cubby put her pen down and shook her aching fingers, which were speckled with ink. She raised her arms above her head and stretched.

"Pens down, right now."

There were four girls in the room, sitting this very last exam of their school life. They had reached the end. Apart from the final prize-giving ceremony in December, none of them would ever wear their uniform again. It was over.

"Hand in your papers, girls," said Miss Merrilee Summers, who had been supervising the examination.

Eight years had passed, yet the cap of red hair was still glossy, and her smile still bright and restrained. With the passing of time, Miss Summers no longer seemed so young and out of place in the school. Partly, of course, because she herself had grown older, and partly because so many of the elderly teachers who had frightened Cubby on her first day had retired, or in some cases died.

One by one the four girls stood up, stamping the pins and needles from their feet, and handed in their booklets to Miss Summers.

"Well done," said Miss Summers, shuffling the papers in a neat pile. "So, girls, now you're free."

Free! They looked at one another with tired grins. It was true. It was hard to believe, but they were free. They were beyond, somewhere outside and beyond. Beyond the battered paperback volume of Thucydides' *History of the Peloponnesian War;* beyond the bodies piled up in the rivers of ancient Sicily; beyond Nicias and Gylippus; beyond teachers and black laced shoes and the ringing of bells, the racing of pens and flapping of turning pages.

It was no longer necessary to think about what Thucydides had written those thousands of years ago on an ancient war. Even their own war, it seemed, was over now. The soldiers fled through broken streets into helicopters and up into the smoky sky across television screens all over the world.

They were free.

"It's over," said Cubby out loud, but really to herself. "It's over."

"I can't believe it," said Martine, now with only the faintest trace of her French accent. She was tall and handsome and led a cryptic and frenzied social life.

"My neck is in agony," said Bethany. Her hair was short now — she'd cut off the plaits one Christmas holidays — but her eyes remained large and she still cried, although not as often.

Miss Summers shook their hands, mouthing good wishes for the future, but they were scarcely aware she was there. As they left the room together, they felt a kind of lightness that was also empty. They never had to think about Thucydides again; that was true. So what would they think about?

"And my shoulders," Bethany moaned, swinging her head from side to side.

"What did you think?" Cubby asked Icara, meaning the examination.

Icara put her pen in her blazer pocket, with a satisfied look on her face. Everyone knew she would do wonderfully well in the exam, in all her exams. She was fanatically interested in her studies — French, Latin, English, history, physics, maths.

She and Cubby remained friends, though somehow Cubby had never been invited back to her house. The judge had married again. He married Mrs. Ellerman the year after Miss Renshaw disappeared. When Icara told Cubby, she had tried not to look surprised, because she could see that Icara did not want her to. But she was very surprised. She did not ask Icara about Amanda, who had left the school that same year and presumably gone off to college, or perhaps overseas. Or perhaps she married. She had disappeared in her own way, just like Miss Renshaw.

"What did you think?" repeated Cubby.

"It was OK," said Icara.

It was by chance, really, that these four — Cubby, Martine, Bethany, and Icara — had found themselves thrown together in their final year, in the advanced ancient history class. In all the years since the eleven little girls had headed out under morning sunshine into the Ena Thompson Memorial Gardens, they had dispersed into different classes and groups as they entered high school, when a great new influx of girls arrived. One class became six; the eleven were spread about; the bond was broken, almost.

But there was a bond. It was a thin, strong bond of shame. After all, they were the girls whose teacher had been murdered on an excursion. Everyone knew that somehow they must be to blame.

Miss Summers clipped off on her high heels to the staff room, and the four girls ambled out to the playground. There was nobody around, as the bell for the end of school had rung an hour ago. Should they just leave? It seemed wrong somehow. There should be some sort of ritual, to remind them what they were doing.

"I guess we could go and tell Miss Baskerville how the exam went," said Cubby.

Miss Baskerville had not retired or died. "Age shall not weary her," Cubby's mother had said, "nor the years condemn."

"Do you think so?" said Bethany with a grimace.

They knew what she meant. They were not altogether confident that Miss Baskerville, deep in her icy office, would want to know how it went.

"Let's just go," said Martine. "Let's get out of here."

So they did. They made their way through the playground to the yellow gate and pushed it open. It swung on its hinges as it had done so many thousands, maybe millions, of times before. But this was the last time. Out they went, one, two, three, four, like astronauts leaving a spaceship, hurtling into the universe.

They wandered into the street, past the empty rubbish bins, the high blocks of units, and the crumbling terrace houses, down past the little stone church, and along the walled laneway where someone had painted WHO KILLED JUANITA? in large, dripping white letters.

"We've got to do something," said Bethany, disconsolate. "We can't just go home. It feels wrong."

It did feel wrong.

"We could get the bus into the city," suggested Cubby, "and have afternoon tea."

"Yes, to celebrate!" said Martine, who spent her weekends going to celebrations of one kind or another.

The bus into town was crowded at that hour, so they had to stand and hang on the railings overhead as it swung up and down the city streets. Usually the girls were hampered by carrying bags full of textbooks and lined paper, but not today. Today all they had were pens in their pockets. They were free.

The bus left them outside a large nineteenth-century building made up of curved arches and overhanging stone flowers. They moved in and out through streams of people with shopping bags and briefcases to their favorite place for afternoon tea, Madame de Pompadour's Continental Café. It was in an underground arcade, between a shop that sold ballet slippers on one side and a magic-supplies center on the other.

One advantage of Madame de Pompadour's Continental Café was that as well as ordinary chairs and tables, it had booths with cushioned benches that they could hide inside and not be seen. They were not supposed to eat in public places in their uniform. *Remember, girls, you are representing the school.* Now the schoolgirls who were no longer schoolgirls slunk into a booth inside the café and collapsed.

"It's over," said Bethany.

"Roger, over and out," agreed Martine.

The walls of Madame de Pompadour's were covered with velvety wallpaper featuring silhouettes of a lady with very high hair, presumably Madame de Pompadour herself.

"Who was Madame de Pompadour, anyway?" Bethany wondered aloud, not for the first time.

"I told you, she was the mistress of the king of France," said Icara, who knew everything. "It wasn't her real name. Her real name was actually Fish. In French, I mean. Poisson."

"What a terrible name," said Martine. "No wonder she changed it." She slumped back against the wallpaper and put her hands out in front of her dramatically. "Nevermore! No more history, ever, ever, ever."

"I like history," said Bethany mildly.

"I hate history," said Martine.

In fact, Martine hated every single subject with equal rage. She was never going to study again in her life, she said. She was going to do something wild. The others, however, did not intend to do anything wild. Icara was going to university to study law. Cubby, too, hoped to go to university, but with no idea of what to study. "I'll do art," she said vaguely. Bethany was going to be an occupational therapist. Nobody knew what that was, and neither did Bethany.

"You know the funny thing about history?" said Cubby, half to herself. "Sometimes I can't quite believe it."

"Can't believe what?" asked Martine, looking around for the waitress. She was hungry.

"That it all ever happened."

"That what happened?" Bethany said with a frown.

"I don't know, all those people. Those ancient Greeks," said Cubby. "Don't you ever wonder, were they real? Did it all really happen? Or is it all just a kind of, I don't know, a hoax."

Martine didn't care if it had happened or not. "I think I will have a crumpet," she decided, reading the paper menu, "with honey and clotted cream."

"I mean, there are just so many people in the world that are supposed to have lived," continued Cubby, unable to let it go. "Millions and millions of people, living and dying. It's sort of unbelievable. How could the world have so many people in it?"

"Well, we wouldn't even know about them," Icara pointed out, "if Thucydides hadn't written it all down. Then it wouldn't matter if they lived or died, would it? We wouldn't care."

Suddenly Bethany made a noise, a kind of cough, as though

something had caught in her throat. She grabbed Cubby's arm and held it hard with her fingers.

"Are you all right?" asked Cubby, alarmed. Was she sick? Was she choking on something?

Bethany shook her head. She raised her hand in the air, pointing, like an actor on stage. Her face turned pink and then white.

They peered out from the booth, to see what she was pointing at. And they saw. There was a woman coming toward them, powering forward relentlessly, like a tidal wave. She was gazing at them with a calm recognition, as though she had been sitting and waiting in Madame de Pompadour's Continental Café all those years, just waiting for them to walk in the door.

It was Miss Renshaw.

NINETEEN

Transformation

"Girls!" said Miss Renshaw. She reached their table and stood before them, unmistakable in her drooping geometric dress. "I knew it was you."

The four girls were as motionless as bricks. Miss Renshaw pulled over a chair and sat herself down, smoothing the familiar springy hair.

"My goodness me," she said. "My goodness me."

The waitress came over with a notepad to take their order, but none of them noticed she was there. She shrugged and strolled back to the cash register.

"Well, haven't you all grown up?" said Miss Renshaw. Her tone was not exactly admiring. "What happened to those funny little girls I used to know? You're all young women now."

Cubby felt her heart beating inside her as though it were banging against the bars of a prison cell. *Let me out! Let me out!*

Bethany was the first to speak, her voice low but triumphant.

"I knew you'd come back," she said. "I always said you would. Didn't I?" She turned to the others. "I always said Miss Renshaw would come back. . . ."

Her voice trailed away.

"Of course I was going to come back," said Miss Renshaw briskly. "Why wouldn't I?"

Why wouldn't she? Cubby saw the four luminous words forming themselves on the blackboard in front of her. In all the years since, she had forced herself not to think about those words. She had refused to. By a great act of will she had wiped the memory from her mind. But the words were still there, hoarsely whispered in her ear.

Not now. Not ever.

It was Martine who said what they were all thinking.

"At school they thought you were dead."

A phone rang. The waitress picked it up and began to murmur into it.

"Did they, now?" said Miss Renshaw. "Dear me. Dead! For heaven's sake. Do I look dead to you?"

They had to admit, Miss Renshaw did not look dead. Her eyes were bright, her face and expression as vivid and lionlike as ever. In fact, she was unchanged. They had changed, all of them, but Miss Renshaw had not.

We shall all be changed, in the twinkling of an eye.

"B-b-but we had a service in the chapel," stammered Cubby. "A memorial service. Because you were dead."

"Oh, not with that dreary old chaplain!" Miss Renshaw groaned theatrically. "You know what, girls? I look forward to the day when we have women ministers in the church, don't you? It'll certainly be a lot more entertaining."

"So what happened?" said Martine, again with that helpful tendency to ask what everyone wanted to know. "Where have you been?"

"Where have I been?" replied Miss Renshaw, raising her eyebrows. "I've been here and there, my dear. Here and there."

Here and there?

"I mean, that day," said Martine doggedly. "Where did you go that day? The day we went down to the gardens?"

"Oh, that dreadful day." Miss Renshaw sat back in her chair and let out a deep breath. "Well, it wasn't so dreadful, really, I suppose, just unexpected. I had no plan, you know, girls, to take off like that. It was all Morgan."

Morgan. Morgan.

"You see, girls, I might as well tell you." Miss Renshaw leaned toward them confidentially. "Morgan's number had come up."

The forbidden name, spoken so casually, so lightly.

"Surely you girls haven't forgotten that barbaric time?" said Miss Renshaw. "The draft? The Vietnam War? Oh, really, as I used to say in the staff room, these children might as well be living in an eighteenth-century convent, for all the interest they take in the world."

Well, of course they knew about the Vietnam War. Although, it was true that they knew a great deal more about the Peloponnesian War in the fifth century BC.

"Morgan was going to be drafted. To go to Vietnam!" Miss Renshaw's shoulders shook, in a mixture of indignation and laughter. "Can you imagine it?"

"But wasn't he . . . ?" Bethany began. "Didn't he . . . ?"

"In the paper," said Cubby. "The paper said that Morgan . . ." She couldn't say it.

"He'd been in prison," said Icara, the realist, speaking for the first time, and her voice was harsh. "He was a convicted criminal. They wouldn't want him in the army."

Miss Renshaw put her head on one side. It was as though she hadn't heard what Icara said.

"Do you remember the weather that morning, girls? It was so fresh, so warm — positively alcoholic. I wasn't really myself. Or perhaps" — she raised a finger at them, posing the question — "I was *more* myself, my true self."

They waited. What could they say?

"It was always Morgan's plan, you know, to disappear into the center of Australia. Even if there was no draft. He wanted to go where nobody could find him, to get away from nuclear war."

Nuclear war?

"He had a camper van, you know. His getaway car," said Miss Renshaw. "So — I don't know, girls, I suppose I went mad.

I thought, yes, I'll go! So we just decided. Just like that. We would leave — we would escape — together."

She closed her eyes for a moment.

"That's why we took you down to the cave. Morgan thought it would give us time to get away. There was another route out of the cave, you see, at the back."

Who had said there was another way out? Someone — one of the Elizabeths? She was right, after all.

"Morgan knew the way," said Miss Renshaw, opening her eyes. "I told you that, remember? Morgan knew all the paths and caves. All the hiding places."

Morgan knew. Cubby felt the familiar, terrible fear, that fear she had felt so many times over the past nine years in recurring nightmares. Morgan, his beard, his smell, his deep, beautiful voice. The cave, the darkness, the moving light — and the hands, all the hands on the rock, reaching upward, beseeching, in those ancient, dusty colors. But how could she remember the hands, when she had never seen them?

"What about us?" Cubby burst out. "You left us there! Weren't you worried about us?"

"Oh, I knew you'd be all right," said Miss Renshaw dismissively. "What could happen to you? You were perfectly safe."

The waitress began to clear the tables, wiping them with a cloth. It was nearly five o'clock. The café would be closing. It was too late to order anything.

"I knew you'd all go back to school," said Miss Renshaw, "and then they'd look for me and then they wouldn't find me and then life would go on."

Tra-la-la, life goes on.

"That's what happened, isn't it?" said Miss Renshaw. "Life went on?"

"I suppose it did," Cubby said dully.

It went on, only it wasn't quite the same. It was never quite the same.

Next to her, Cubby became aware of Icara trembling. She had her hands wedged under her thighs, and she was staring down intently at the place mat in front of her, with its cheap drawing of Madame de Pompadour. Was she having a fit? Cubby had read about people having fits—there was that book, *The Idiot*—and that prince—what was his name? Russian names were so difficult—and why was everyone a prince? It didn't make sense. . . .

"So what did you do?" asked Martine. "Where did you end up going? And what happened to Morgan?"

Morgan.

"Morgan," said Miss Renshaw, "was a fascinating man. His life took some strange turns. For a while, girls, he would only eat rice, nothing but. We kept a giant sack of it on the kitchen floor. And then, at one point, would you believe, he even became a warlock."

"You mean, like a witch?" said Bethany, with her large, round eyes.

"Something like that," agreed Miss Renshaw. "It wasn't easy, I can tell you. I don't suppose you little girls can imagine what it's like to live with a man who thinks he's a warlock."

"We're not so little now," said Icara.

She's crazy, thought Cubby. Quite mad, just as Cubby's mother had always maintained. Only they'd been too little, too inexperienced, to recognize it.

"But what happened to him?" persisted Martine. "Where is he now?"

Miss Renshaw paused.

"He died," she said.

"Drugs," said Icara.

Miss Renshaw just looked at her.

"You really have to try to be more sympathetic, Icara," she said. "Or people won't like you."

But I like her, thought Cubby.

"I like her," said Cubby out loud.

"He had cancer," said Miss Renshaw, ignoring Cubby. "And then, with his principles, he wouldn't go to a doctor."

"What principles?" asked Bethany.

"Modern medicine has brought nothing but trouble," said Miss Renshaw. "It creates more diseases than it cures. You girls should think about that."

There was another pause.

"I've thought about it now," said Icara.

"Anyway," continued Miss Renshaw, "he wouldn't see a doctor, but he found a marvelous healer just outside Lismore who treated him with herbs. I had to cook them up twice a day into a kind of tea. Brilliant stuff. Life-giving."

"But he died," Cubby couldn't help pointing out.

"Well, I guess his number was up," said Icara.

"Icara, there is something intensely unsympathetic about

you," said Miss Renshaw. "We are talking about a man's death here."

"Did he write any more poems?" asked Martine, changing the subject.

"Some," said Miss Renshaw. "But he became more interested in politics."

"I suppose you could write poems about politics," said Bethany doubtfully.

Miss Renshaw stood up.

"I must go, girls. I just couldn't resist coming over, seeing you like that. I hope I haven't given you too much of a shock."

She smoothed down her springy hair and smiled broadly. Then she leaned over and patted Cubby on the shoulder.

"Don't look so stricken, Cubby. Courage. To strive, to seek, to find!"

"And not to yield," said Cubby automatically, for she knew the poem well.

"That's the spirit."

And Miss Renshaw was gone. For the second time. Gone.

TWENTY

Schoolgirl Flying

THE CAFÉ WAS CLOSING. The waitress tapped her watch and gestured at the door. They had to leave, having eaten nothing.

"Let's get out of here," said Icara.

They struggled out of the cushioned booth, dazed, and left Madame de Pompadour's Continental Café, heading out onto the sloping plaza of the city.

"That was strange," said Bethany.

The bells of the post office clock were chiming and the summer evening began to fall, the dying light tunneled in by the high bank buildings that rose up on either side. Automatically, they put their hats on their heads.

"Wait till we tell the others," said Martine. "They won't believe it. Miss Renshaw came back!"

They won't believe it. Nobody would believe it. Did it really happen?

"I wonder if she'll go to school," said Bethany. "You know, and walk in the gate and say, 'Hello, everyone, it's me!'"

She stopped for a moment, staggering into Martine. Her face was still very pink, but she didn't cry.

"She won't go back there," said Icara definitely. "She wouldn't dare."

They passed a newspaper kiosk. A crowd had gathered around it, picking up papers. There were posters with shouting black headlines. But the girls didn't stop to see what the news was. Perhaps they remembered the day when Morgan's ghostly head had appeared across the front page, in a threatening mist of ink.

"What's that smell?" said Martine, lifting her nose like a bear.

It was a rich smell, but not of flowers. Then they saw a man with little bunches of rosemary for sale, standing on the corner.

"It's Remembrance Day," said Icara.

So it was. November 11. Because of their exam, they had hardly noticed. They hadn't been involved in any of the usual school rituals, the two minutes' silence and the singing of hymns for dead soldiers. Remembrance Day.

"The Day of the Dead," said Martine.

They were close to the cenotaph now, just outside the

shadowy porticos of the post office. A helmeted soldier in bronze stood at one end of a long box with a stone wreath laid on it, and a bronze sailor stood at the other end, both staring blindly out into the city in opposite directions. TO OUR GLORIOUS DEAD was engraved in the stone on one side of the box, and on the other, LEST WE FORGET. Yellow roses lay at the great glowing feet of the soldier, next to his resting gun.

"It looks like a coffin," said Bethany.

"It is a coffin," said Icara. "*Cenotaph* means 'empty tomb' in Greek. That's what it is."

A hot wind blew down from the hill, carrying dust into their eyes and hair, like cinders.

"You know what was really strange?" said Martine.

What? What was really strange?

"Miss Renshaw was wearing the same dress."

Ah.

"You mean . . ." said Bethany.

"Exactly the same dress as the day she disappeared," said Martine.

They looked at one another carefully. Martine was right. Miss Renshaw was wearing that same crimson dress with its geometrical pattern of interlocking squares and triangles and its drooping sleeves. The dress she had been wearing that last day, in the Ena Thompson Memorial Gardens.

"Yes, she was," said Cubby slowly.

"It wasn't just her clothes," said Martine. "But her—I mean, she looked exactly the same. Didn't she?"

"Do you think . . . ?" Bethany began, and then stopped.

"That she was a ghost?" Martine finished the sentence for her.

"A ghost? Just because she was wearing the same dress?" Icara rolled her eyes. "People do wear clothes more than once, you know."

"Nobody wears dresses like that anymore," retorted Martine, "not even a teacher."

"But if she was a ghost," said Bethany, perplexed, anxious, "then it doesn't make sense. All those things she told us, about Morgan and—and all those things. It doesn't make sense."

"No, that's right. It doesn't make any sense," said Icara impatiently. "It's ridiculous. She's not a ghost. There are no such things as ghosts. When you're dead, you're dead."

"Yes . . ." Bethany admitted, but she did not sound at all sure.

"And she definitely wasn't dead," said Icara. "Was she? Did she look dead?"

Bethany thought about it. *No, Miss Renshaw did not look dead.*

"So she wasn't a ghost," she said, pleading.

"No, she wasn't," said Icara. "I was wrong. I was the one that said she was dead, and she's not. She's not dead. She's alive."

They walked on, away from the cenotaph and the plaza, on to George Street.

"I think she was a ghost," said Martine.

"Well, you're wrong," said Icara.

At the end of the road they could see a sliver of the ocean, that same curling Pacific Ocean that had carried Captain Cook across the world in his little wooden boat. It shone like a thousand mirrors, mirror upon mirror upon mirror, like star upon star in the sky.

"Let's run," said Martine, who was intending to go wild after all. "Let's run down to the water."

They ran. With one hand on their hats to stop them blowing away and the other outstretched, they sprinted. They ran to the edges of the earth, four schoolgirls for the last time.

They ran until they reached the end of the wide street and crossed over to the row of creaking wharves, the newsstands, the red-eyed seagulls and the smell of fish, and darted through the afternoon crowds to the lapping water. The air was full of sounds—ropes splashing, gulls crying, and the soft bells of signaling boats.

Catching their breath, they leaned together on the cold iron railing, gazing out at the ocean. Cubby stood slightly apart, next to Icara. Her heart was beating hard, and her eyes were thick with thoughts.

She knew Miss Renshaw was dead, whatever Icara now said. Cubby knew it. Morgan had murdered her in that low, dark cave eight years ago. Cubby knew it now, without any doubt, because of something she alone had seen that afternoon, that no one else had even noticed.

It was when Miss Renshaw had stood up in the café to say good-bye. She'd leaned over Cubby and touched her arm, and the collar of her geometrical dress had opened like a boulder rolling from the mouth of a tomb.

There, nestled around Miss Renshaw's neck on a string of

black leather, was the tear-shaped amber bead: the necklace that was safely wrapped up in a police evidence bag in a warehouse of unsolved crimes. Cubby saw it, unbroken, hanging around Miss Renshaw's neck in Madame de Pompadour's Continental Café, with the little insect still inside it, trapped forever in the bright golden honey of time.

And at that moment, Cubby realized she was not going to turn into the person she had thought she would become. There was something inside her head now that would make her a different person, although she scarcely understood what it was.

And we shall all be changed in the twinkling of an eye.

Miss Renshaw was dead. And yet she was not dead. She had spoken to them; she had tossed back her springy hair; she had touched Cubby's arm. Was nobody, then, really dead? Was Morgan, too, alive and well, drinking herbs in a hidden hamlet in the hills above Lismore? Perhaps nobody was dead. Not even Ronald Ryan, hanged in prison on that faraway February day. . . .

The four girls stared out at the blue-gray rocking water of the Pacific Ocean, each with their own secret thoughts. They were too big for the pond now. Soon they would be caught up in a net and tossed high into that open sea. They would strike out and flap their fins bravely through the rolling waves.

What would happen to them? They might struggle in the cold depths, with only the occasional glimpse of the sunlit world above. They might even die, their tiny fragile bones sinking to the ocean floor to turn slowly into grains of sand. Or they might prosper and grow sleek and strong, and shine like silver.

That afternoon, they felt no astonishment at any of it. Perhaps a butterfly, too, is unimpressed by its transformation from those wormlike beginnings. Why shouldn't it crawl out from the darkness, spread its tiny wings, and fly off into the windy mystery of the trees? The grub lies quietly in its soft cocoon, silent, thinking. It knows everything.

A ferry was just leaving the wharf. It sounded its horn and moved through the harbor like a swan, toward an uncertain horizon. And although it was the end of the day, for all of them it felt like morning.

When the golden day is done,

Through the closing portal,

Child and garden, flower and sun,

Vanish all things mortal.

—"Night and Day"
ROBERT LOUIS STEVENSON

Author's Note

The Golden Day is a novel set in Sydney in 1967, ending in 1975, about a group of schoolgirls whose teacher bizarrely goes missing on a school excursion, apparently murdered.

The idea began at least thirty years ago, when I saw Charles Blackman's wonderful *Floating Schoolgirl* in the National Gallery in Canberra. It's a painting of a surreal schoolgirl in hat and tunic floating above the city in the darkness — like an image from an urban *Picnic at Hanging Rock,* the iconic Australian film about schoolgirls who go missing on a bush picnic. The flying child may be frightened, but she's also brimming with the joy of a secret life.

That painting was the seed, but as with any book, there were many others. Some were grim — the schoolgirl from New South Wales shot dead in the chapel by the artist Lennie Lawson in 1962; the disappearance of Juanita Nielsen from Kings Cross, Sydney, in 1975; the murder of nine-year-old Samantha Knight in 1986. Then there was the great classic of Australian schoolgirl life, Henry Handel Richardson's *The Getting of Wisdom;* the gentle, hidden poetry of John Shaw Neilson; Freud's notion of the "mystic writing pad"; and the melancholy abandoned pleasure park by the Lane Cove River, known as Fairyland. But the greatest debt is to Charles Blackman's many astonishing, lush depictions of schoolgirls — enchanting, disturbing, and endlessly evocative.

Of course, pulsing beneath it all must be the memory of my own Sydney school days, however transformed into fiction. The story is told essentially from the point of view of eleven little girls, who spend their days under the protection of an almost entirely female private educational institution in the late 1960s, at a time of overwhelming social changes that are both robustly embraced and robustly rejected by the various adults about them.

The little girls watch, wonder, respond, change, and grow — and then they're gone, forever. This element of the story, I suppose, is at least partly autobiographical! But you can rest assured that all my own teachers came home safe and sound in the end. . . .